BEATEN BUT NOT CONQUERED

Briggs managed to shove his attacker off and roll to the right. But as he did, something that felt like a twenty-ton lead weight slammed into his testicles. The excruciating pain bounced off the inside of his skull, echoing within his head as if it were the Grand Canyon.

Briggs swung out blindly, his right hook connecting with something soft. A split instant later two hammer blows smashed into his side, cracking at least one of his ribs with an audible pop.

"Christ," Briggs swore, falling backward.

He finally saw his assailant. He was an exceedingly well-built Japanese man, barefoot and wearing black pajamas. And the man was coming at him again. . . .

DYNAMIC NEW LEADERS IN MEN'S ADVENTURE!

THE MAGIC MAN #2:
THE GAMOV FACTOR (1252, $2.50)
by David Bannerman
With Brezhnev terminally ill, the West needs an agent in place to control the outcome of the race to replace him. And there's no one better suited for the job than THE MAGIC MAN!

THE WARLORD (1189, $3.50)
by Jason Frost
The world's gone mad with disruption. Isolated from help, the survivors face a state in which law is a memory and violence is the rule. Only one man is fit to lead the people, a man raised among the Indians and trained by the Marines. He is Erik Ravensmith, THE WARLORD—a deadly adversary and a hero of our times.

THE WARLORD #2: THE CUTTHROAT (1308, $2.50)
by Jason Frost
Though death sails the Sea of Los Angeles, there is only one man who will fight to save what is left of California's ravaged paradise. His name is THE WARLORD—and he won't stop until the job is done!

THE WARLORD #3: BADLAND (1437, $2.50)
by Jason Frost
His son has been kidnapped by his worst enemy and THE WARLORD must fight a pack of killers to free him. Getting close enough to grab the boy will be nearly impossible—but then so is living in this tortured world!

Available wherever paperbacks are sold, or order direct from the Publisher. Send cover price plus 50¢ per copy for mailing and handling to Zebra Books, Dept. 1593, 475 Park Avenue South, New York, N.Y. 10016. DO NOT SEND CASH.

CALL OF HONOR

By David Bannerman

ZEBRA BOOKS
KENSINGTON PUBLISHING CORP.

ZEBRA BOOKS

are published by

Kensington Publishing Corp.
475 Park Avenue South
New York, NY 10016

Copyright © 1985 by David Bannerman

All rights reserved. No part of this book may be reproduced in any form or by any means without the prior written consent of the Publisher, excepting brief quotes used in reviews.

First printing: May 1985

Printed in the United States of America

For Laurie

PROLOGUE

1964

Soshi Taranaga entered the tiny Shinto temple at the back of his home, sank gratefully to his knees on the mat, and bowed deeply: once, twice, three times.

It had been too long since he had been back on his island. Too many days and weeks of Tokyo's modern filth to cloud his pure vision.

Everything had changed since the glory days of the 1930s and the early 1940s when Japan's rising sun had shone so brightly that the heathen were blinded by its vision.

Everything had changed in Japan as well as out here, in the South Pacific islands that had once been Japan's supreme accomplishment.

Of course, even Taranaga, who was now forty-eight years old and could still remember the old ways, had to admit that some the changes were for the better.

Now, instead of months to travel from Tokyo to Truk Islands, the journey was done by air in hours.

But the greatest advantage to the changes that had been wrought — mostly by the Americans — since the war, was the ability for anyone of even moderate intelligence to accumulate wealth.

And with wealth, Taranaga thought, a man could be safe from the prying eyes of people who would do him harm.

As usual, Taranaga had changed out of his western-styled clothes the moment he'd arrived at his island stronghold. Now he wore the traditional Japanese kimono, spotlessly white stockings, and sandals.

The first order of business had been to check on the operation of the copra processing plant which was on the far side of the big island.

The second was accomplished here in his private temple, where he purified his mind for the third task.

Here in the temple, Taranaga once more became Japanese — but Japanese as his people had been before and during the war. Proud; in many respects, inflexible. But in all respects, very strong.

Here in the temple, Taranaga could feel the strength coming to his sinews, making them as steel cords. He could feel strength of purpose coming into his mind as well. Strength to continue with what he knew in his Japanese heart was good, and correct.

In 1940, there would have been absolutely no question of his actions. But now the world was different; now the world demanded stealth and secrecy that his money, thankfully, could buy for him.

The American magazine, *Time,* had called

Taranaga the rising star on Japan's horizon.

Electronics would be the salvation of Japanese world power, the story had read. This time, instead of guns and ships and planes, the Japanese would become powers in the American dollar, the German mark, the British pound.

Taranaga was a short man, even as Japanese go, and very slight of build. His was a round face, his eyes traditionally Japanese, his complexion flawless and dark, his fingers long and delicately shaped.

The only hint of cruelty that could be seen outwardly were his lips, and the corners of his mouth. Someone had once called them the lips of a sadist.

He had to smile. It had been going on now for years — since 1937, when he'd been a young soldier of twenty-one stationed here in the islands.

Taranaga let his mind roam back to those less-complicated times for just a moment, then he let himself out of his temple, went through the large house, and headed around back up into the hills on the path.

He had been coming this way now for a long time — since 1937. Intellectually he understood that someday this would all end, that there would be no further reason for his visits.

And Kobi and Heidinori would no longer be necessary. He had sworn both men to secrecy when it had become clear what would have to be done. They had stuck with their duties, as good samurai might. They were loyal and understood the old ways. They alone, here on the island, were from the war. And it was here they would remain so long as their job existed.

After a while the path steepened, and Taranaga

began to perspire lightly. The afternoon was lovely; only a few puffy clouds marred an otherwise perfectly clear blue sky.

At one point the path came very near the edge of the cliffs on the island's eastern side, and he could feel the cool tradewind, and see the reef well offshore that protected them.

He wiped his forehead, and looked up the path. The reef protected them from the outside, and the native fears and superstitions had protected his secret above for all these years now. Their fears and superstitions, plus Taranaga's largesse, he thought.

He continued slowly up the hill, his heart beginning to pound in his chest, now that he was close, as it always did.

Over the years he had enjoyed coming back here. Even more so in recent times, because of the distressing way in which Tokyo and most of Japan was progressing. Here was a haven.

The path suddenly flattened, and around a sharp bend it angled off to the north. Taranaga stepped off the path, down a short incline, and then stepped behind some bushes into a large cave hollowed out of the side of the mountain.

This had been done by the Japanese army engineers during the war. The invasion had been inevitable; they'd all known it. And they had spent years fortifying as many South Pacific islands as they could get their hands on. This was one of the fortifications that had never been used.

Unfortunate for the Japanese army, Taranaga thought, but very fortunate for him.

Ten feet from the entrance, Taranaga knew that

something had gone wrong—something very drastic.

In the still, damp air of the cave, he could smell the cloying, sweet odor of death. Someone here was dead.

His thin lips compressed and his eyes hardened as he slowly moved deeper into the cave.

Kobi Suzu lay on his back, most of his chest blown away; flies swarmed on the gaping wound. He had been dead for days. Perhaps weeks. He had been shot in the chest at close range.

Taranaga, his entire body shaking now, thrumming like a plucked string, stepped carefully around his old friend's rotting body, and through the low doorway that separated the outer chamber from the labyrinth beyond.

Heidinori Matsura lay on his side, in a seeming embrace with the old woman. A pistol lay beside them. The side of Heidi's head was blown away; blood, bits of bone, and white brain matter were splattered across the cave floor.

A lot of blood lay beside the woman. Shaking with rage, Taranaga stepped around them, until he could see that just before Heidi had died, he had apparently cut her throat. Then she had shot him in the head at close range.

He let his eyes look up. The cage she had been kept in was open. Three of the bars had been worked loose and taken out of their concrete slots. There was blood around the base of the bars.

He looked back at Heidi and the woman, and then out at Kobi's lifeless body.

She had shot and killed Kobi. Then Heidi had overcome her, had slit her throat, and as she lay there struggling with the last of her life fluid ebbing out of her, she'd fired her pistol into his head at point-blank range.

It was very difficult for Taranaga to keep himself in control. His entire world had been shattered by this one monstrous act.

He reached down and rolled Heidi away from the woman. Then he stepped back and shook his head, the tears coming to his eyes. A waste. Such a terrible waste, with no one to make reparations.

He stepped back into the outer chamber, and then up the concealed entrance, where he sat down crosslegged just below the path, at a point where he could see the ocean.

It was late afternoon. Before long it would be night. Then he would take the woman's body far up into the hills where he would bury it.

For Heidi and Kobi, there would be an honorable cremation. Later, their ashes would be spread on the wind, so that they could finally be free to roam the oceans of the world.

Freedom, Taranaga thought. They would be free. Old friends, who had served him well. They truly deserved the freedom they had achieved.

For him, though, there still was the war. It would go on for a very long time, he thought, as the glimmerings of a plan began to form in his mind.

After his affairs had been settled here, after he had spent enough time to thoroughly cleanse himself, he would return to Tokyo.

He had already made slightly more than a million dollars, American. It was time to go into business in a much larger way. It was time for him to make a major fortune, at the expense of the Americans, with which he could wage his war against them. Against the white man!

He was shaking with rage again. It was impossible to control his emotions.

He jumped up, shaking his fists against the sky and the sea, and screamed: *"Banzai! Banzai! Banzai!"*

One

1984

The BOAC flight from Washington, D.C., touched down at London's Heathrow Airport just a few minutes after three on an overcast July afternoon, and Donald O'Meara (Briggs to his friends) wondered why the hell he was coming back like this.

The last time he had been in London it had been with the sharp memory of Oumi Pavlacek's death. The one man on this earth who had most been like a father to him was buried in the Highgate cemetery.

Most of the other émigrés were dead as well. There was really nothing for him to return to. Other than Sylvia Hume, of course, but he preferred not to think about her, at least not until it became absolutely necessary.

Briggs was a tall man, on the husky side, with Irish-red hair, sparkling blue eyes, and a lilt in his voice when he wanted it there. He was a passable tenor, and at forty-two he was in the peak of his physical condition, although just lately he had been drinking entirely too much Irish whiskey.

On the flight over, the stewardess named Susy had switched positions with one of the other stews so that she could serve the man in 27A, who had been so nice to the little old lady so afraid of flying—and who was a definite hunk.

Briggs had been aware of her attraction, and before they had touched down, he had found out the hotel she'd be staying at for the next forty-eight hours. He promised he'd make the time to drop by for a drink.

The only way to fight fire, he had justified his move, was with fire. Sylvia would understand perfectly, even if she wouldn't approve.

After they had landed and the boarding tunnel had been connected, Briggs helped the old lady who had been his seatmate with her carry-on bags, then collected his single case, and left the plane, with a wink for the stew.

He was processed through customs with no delays, and within fifteen minutes of the time the 747 had touched down on British soil, he was outside at the cab stands, sniffing the London air.

No fuss was to be made of his arrival. He had reservations at Browns, a very Victorian, very proper old hotel on Dover Street, and tomorrow sometime he would be picked up and driven out to Sir Roger Hume's residence outside the city.

After his reception there, he would be briefed. "Nothing much, we're told," Rudyard Howard, his boss at the State Department, had informed him.

"Then send someone else," Briggs had replied. It had been too long since he had been back to London. His return would open too many old wounds, he figured.

"They've asked for our help on this one, Donald," Howard had said. He was a very short, stocky man with a bald head. He had always reminded Briggs of a bulldog. He and Howard had never gotten along, although the man's wife was a wonderful woman.

"And they asked for me, specifically?"

"Hope-Turner did."

"At Sir Roger Hume's suggestion, no doubt. Which in turn was at his daughter's urging. Christ on a cross, Rudyard, don't you see what they're trying to do to me?"

"No," Howard said dryly. "What exactly are *they* trying to do to you?"

"Marry me off, for God's sake."

Howard grinned. "You could do worse, although why Sylvia would ever want you is totally beyond me."

"Perhaps she thinks I'm cute," Briggs had said, backing quickly out of Howard's office.

In the end, of course, he had accepted. There had been no real alternative. He *was* a special operative for the U.S. State Department's special intelligence section, and it was his job. He knew, though, that the task was probably one that was considered to be totally impossible, where an expendable man was needed, because those were the jobs he always got.

By all rights he should have been dead several times over by now. But Briggs had a habit of coming up on his feet after being tossed from a long distance up—and was known as the "magic man" because of it.

He got a cab, told the driver his hotel, and sat back as they headed away from the airport.

Lord, it was bringing back a lot of memories being here like this. His gut tightened. He could not help but think back years to when he was a young boy, living in London with his mother and his uncle in a small flat.

It had been in the late forties. He had come home from school to find his mother's brutally mutilated body lying in their apartment. It had been the Russian NKVD agents in London. They had sent their team out to eliminate Briggs' mother as well as his uncle, who had been doing a little work in the eastern zone of Germany.

He could see the dark stairwell. He could hear the whimpering sound that had puzzled him at first, until he realized it had been coming from his own throat.

He had been a wounded little animal alone in London's Soho district, when he had shown up on Oumi Pavlacek's doorstep.

The war had just been over, and the district was filled with émigrés from the communist areas. Albanians, Rumanians, Hungarians, and Poles had one thing in common—their hate of Russia.

Naturally MI9, and later the British Secret Intelligence Service, was very interested in them. Their networks, that during the war had worked against the Nazis, now worked against the communists.

Briggs, as a young, impressionable boy, had been

plunged into this world.

He had been taught Russian so that he could speak it like a native. He had been taught tradecraft: codes, radio work, safe-houses, drop boxes, tails and being tailed.

And he had been taught to fight. Then to kill. His first hit had been a Russian operative working in London. Briggs had barely been in his teens, but he had dispatched the KGB operative with a skill that was frightening.

From that moment, this training by the émigrés had gone into full swing. Decades of experiences, covering three-quarters of Europe, was lavished on the boy.

When he was fifteen he was given his stiletto. At one time it had belonged to the Czar of Russia. Later, its jeweled handle gone, it was stolen from a museum and given to the star pupil, its handle wrapped with waxed cord. The perfect killing weapon. Silent. Not too terribly messy if it was used correctly.

It had become a friend . . . or, rather, it had become a grim companion that had gotten Briggs out of more than one tight spot in his life.

A lot of Russian blood had been spilled because of its needle point and razor-sharp edges.

Riding now in the cab, Briggs unconsciously patted his suitcase in which the blade, along with his escape kit, had ridden. Besides the stiletto, Briggs always made sure he had about five thousand in U.S. dollars, along with a half-dozen sets of passports and identifications — all perfectly valid, but for six different men answering descriptions that Briggs could assume.

It had been the final bit of tradecraft that Oumi and Vatra and the others had bestowed upon him before he had left England.

Too many killings had been occurring in London for Scotland Yard's taste. It had become a political embarrassment for Number 10 Downing Street. Someone had to be sacrificed. And it had been Briggs.

He had run to the United States, of course. There really was no other place. And over the years he had talked his way into a number of jobs, none of which had lasted more than a couple of years.

He had once studied for a week and a half at the Denver Public Library, and then had applied for and gotten a job as chief engineer on a Denver water project, where a tunnel was being punched through the mountains to bring drinking water to the city from the opposite side of the continental divide.

A couple of years into the project, someone had happened to check Briggs's credentials, out of curiosity sparked by his doing an excellent job. He was found out and had had to run.

He worked as a radio announcer for a time, a rancher—and had almost gotten married—and had finally ended up in Hollywood directing a string of "B" movies.

The last had been a job with a little flare. He had learned the finer arts of make-up and of making oneself appear to be someone completely different.

But he had been less alone during his years of training than he had thought. He had been watched by Sir Roger Hume, an old-school member of parliament and head of the Ministry Council on Foreign Affairs, which was the Secret Intelligence Service's watchdog committee. Sir Roger had been a desk man in the service for a time, and had kept his hand in. He was a man vitally interested in everything the service did.

For some reason, that even Sir Roger had never properly been able to explain, he had become interested in Briggs. He had watched the young man grow into an exceedingly well-trained, highly dangerous operative.

He had watched when Briggs had gone to America. And with his contacts there, he had kept tabs on Briggs.

Sir Roger and Briggs's boss at State, Rudyard Howard, were old friends. They went back to before the war, to when Sir Roger's wife was still alive.

Sir Roger's only daughter, Sylvia, who was now a lovely, dark-haired beauty of twenty-six, who remained on the family estate to help her father, and who was madly in love with Briggs, thought of Rudyard Howard as Uncle Rudy. They were very close, which made it all the more uncomfortable for Briggs, who had very confused feelings about Sylvia.

"Browns, you said it was, guv'ner?" the cabby asked over his shoulder.

"That's right. Dover Street," Briggs said.

Whenever he thought about Sylvia Hume, it put him into a light sweat. He was from the wrong side of the tracks. He had no family, and even if he had they'd be poor Irish. Whereas she was from the

British upper crust. She had been born with the proverbial silver spoon in her mouth. For her there should be more than some . . . operative.

Her father saw it that way; Rudyard Howard saw it that way — but she didn't. She was in love.

Besides, Briggs told himself, he was a bachelor. He did not want to be tied down to one woman. And in rare moments, sometimes very early in the morning, with the sun just coming up, he'd sit alone and think about how different things could have been had his life been normal.

As it was, he knew that he did not want the commitment of a wonderful woman such as Sylvia Hume, because he would forever have to be worried about her while he was out on an assignment. Someday, someone would come after her as a way of getting to him. It had happened countless times before to other operatives. He did not think he could stand the pain. Although, as it was, the pain of not having her was nearly as bad as he could stand.

Browns was a lovely old hotel. Briggs had never been there before, but Travel Section had made the booking and had promised that it would be nice, that he would like it.

They were right. It was nice and he did like it.

After he had unpacked his bags, he sent his suit down to be pressed, and then got dressed in a sports jacket and went to the bar where he ordered himself a neat Irish whiskey.

The barman showed only a faint flicker of surprise, but he served the drink. The Irish were not overly welcome here, but Briggs's accent, at the moment, was obviously very American. He was a Yank.

There was a telephone at the end of the bar, and he used it to telephone the Durrants Hotel on George Street.

For just a moment, he had hesitated, thinking that he should instead telephone Sylvia. But then he went ahead with it. He was not going to catch himself in any kind of a trap, no matter how much it hurt.

"Susan Mercator," he told the hotel operator.

A moment later the connection was made, and a young woman answered.

"Hello, Susan?" Briggs asked.

"No, just a minute," the girl said. He could hear her shouting, and then the stewardess was on the line.

"Hello?"

"Susy, this is Donald O'Meara. Twenty-seven A. Or have you forgotten already?"

"I never forget a face . . . like yours," she said, her voice soft.

"How about dinner?"

"I'd love it."

"Can you be ready by . . ." Briggs looked at his watch. It was nearly six. "By seven?"

"Make it six thirty," she said. "I'll be waiting in the bar. It's nice and quiet."

"See you then," Briggs said, and he hung up and went back to his drink. When he was finished he ordered another, and took it up to his room. His suit had just been returned, and his second pair of shoes had been shined.

He dressed in his suit, shaved again, but before he

put on his jacket he glanced at his stiletto. Then he decided against it.

On assignment he never went anywhere without it. He wasn't on assignment yet. Tomorrow that would start. But even Howard had said this one would be routine . . . whatever that meant.

Susan Mercator had looked lovely in her BOAC flight attendant's uniform. But she was stunning in her white, low-cut cocktail dress. She had evidently spent some time at the beach, because her skin was tanned, and what he could see of her breasts — which was most of them — was a soft brown as well.

She was a tall girl, somewhat on the thin side, but with an athletic grace. Her eyes were wide and very green, her face round, and her nose petite. Her lips were full and sensuous.

It was obvious to Briggs as soon as he sat down with her that she wanted to take him to bed. Usually, he'd be turned off; but this time, he was amused, and somewhat flattered. He was forty-two; this girl was in her very early twenties. What could she see in him?

"What took you so long?" she asked, after they had ordered drinks.

Briggs smiled. "Look," he said, "do you really want to go out to dinner, or would you rather eat in."

She nodded. She was practically panting already.

"I imagine your place is filled with girls — the other stews?"

Again she nodded.

"Then it's my place," he said.

She started to rise, but Briggs held her back. "Let's have a drink first, Susy."

She suddenly realized that she had been making a fool of herself, and her face turned red. She sat down. "Oh Christ," she said.

Briggs held her hands in his. "Don't worry about it. You're a beautiful woman, and I'm damned flattered that you find me so attractive."

"Honestly?" she asked. "You don't think I'm too . . . forward?"

"Of course not."

Their drinks came and Briggs made a toast. "To us and a one-night holiday."

"You're leaving tomorrow?" she asked.

"I'm afraid so. First thing in the morning, actually. I've a bit of work to do."

She sat back, a wry expression coming to her lips. "Then this is to be nothing more than a one-night stand."

"I'm sorry, Susy, I truly am. If you'd rather not . . ." He let it trail off.

"Don't be silly," she said. She toasted him back. "One night is better than no knights," she said, accenting the *K* on the second word.

They went to dinner, after all, at the Connaught Hotel on Carlos Place. It was one of the best kitchens in all of London, and they both relaxed during the excellent meal.

All through the dinner, and then afterwards, when they were walking hand in hand back toward his hotel, Briggs felt like a heel — twice over. Once because of Sylvia (he just couldn't get her out of his mind), and the second because of the girl he was with. Susy was more lonely and frightened than anything else; she wanted someone to hold back the goblins more than she wanted sex.

At one point, Briggs had decided he would send her back to her hotel in a cab, but she would have none of it when the time came. She started to cry, and in the end he brought her upstairs, where they showered together and got into the wide bed.

"It's not always like this," she said, when they were lying together. "I mean, I don't make it a practice of seducing all my passengers."

"I hope not."

She giggled. "It would be interesting though . . ."

Briggs reached over and kissed the nipple of her left breast, cutting her off in mid-sentence.

"Oh," she said in a small voice, her back arching slightly to meet his lips.

Briggs smiled down at her. She wanted love. Someone to hold her. Sooner or later she'd find the right man, who'd want to hold her for a long time. He hoped it would be sooner.

She wanted to rush through it, but Briggs slowed the pace, caressing her beautifully formed breasts, kissing the soft round of her belly, her knees, the insides of her thighs.

She quivered slightly as he moved across her body; her eyes were closed, her lips slightly parted.

"Susy," Briggs said softly. "Susy."

She opened her eyes and looked up at him. There was a desperation there.

"Take a deep breath now," he said softly. "Relax."

"I . . . I don't know."

Christ, he told himself. It was like going to bed with a child, almost. But she *was* a woman.

"Easy," he said. He kissed her neck, and then her lips, as he slowly entered her.

She rose quickly to meet him, her hips moving, her hands on his back, her legs wrapped tightly around his waist.

He didn't move for a long time, waiting until she settled down; then, looking into her eyes, he slowly began making love to her. Their breathing and their rhythms finally matched, and at the end it was very good.

Two

Tunbridge-Wells, also known as Royal Tunbridge-Wells, was on the Sussex border about thirty-five miles southeast of London.

A dark green Jaguar sedan and a driver showed up at his hotel shortly before noon, to take him out to Sir Roger's home just outside the municipal borough of Kent.

Susy had gone back to her own hotel a bit after 10 **a.m**, dreamy-eyed, and ready, she'd said innocently, to stay awake forever so she would never forget what had happened between them.

Briggs especially felt like a heel this morning — not only because of the young stew, but because he'd also be facing Sylvia Hume sometime today.

The long ride out into the countryside was calming, though. The driver was a large, taciturn man, apparently not given to idle conversation. Either that or he had orders not to say a word to Briggs. Which was just as well. It left Briggs to his own thoughts.

It was a lovely day. Hardly a cloud in the sky, warm temperatures, not too much humidity—unusual for England at any time of the year.

On the way out, Briggs thought about the work he had done for the American State Department over the two years since he had begun with them. He had been back to the Soviet Union three times. He wondered where they would be sending him now.

Howard's advice that this would be an easy assignment stuck in his ears. The man had never overestimated a situation, and Briggs did not think he would underestimate one either.

But, if the assignment was so minor, why send him?

They passed through Tunbridge-Wells, and soon afterwards turned off the highway onto a rutted, bumpy dirt road. A long white fence ran along either side of the driveway. Sir Roger raised racing horses, and trained them, with Sylvia's help.

Briggs sat forward. In the distance, outlined against the blue sky at the top of the hill, was a lone horse and rider. It was Sylvia; he was certain of it.

"Stop here," he told the driver.

"Sir?" the man asked over his shoulder.

"I said, stop here, man. Now!"

"Yessir," the driver said, bringing the Jaguar to a halt.

Briggs jumped out and went to the fence, where he waved up at Sylvia.

But she just sat there.

Briggs waved again. "Sylvia! he called, cupping his mouth.

She turned and disappeared over the hill, leaving Briggs standing below, with his arm raised.

After a minute, he turned and went back to the car.

"Ready now, sir?"

"Sure," Briggs said. He wasn't going to let this get him down, he told himself. He wanted Sylvia to have no hold on him. He certainly could not expect to have a hold on her.

Sir Roger Hume, was tall for his age (he would admit to no more than fifty-five, but Briggs was certain the old man had to be in his late sixties), and stood ramrod straight.

"A mark of breeding and upbringing," he was fond of saying.

He had a thick shock of silver hair, a hawklike nose, and a jutting, angular chin. His eyes were wide, and the most penetrating blue of any Briggs had ever looked into.

He stood on the broad front veranda of the large house as the Jaguar came up the long driveway. He was not alone. For a moment Briggs did not recognize the other man, although he was certain he knew him.

When they were closer, he suddenly realized that it was Stuart Hope-Turner, head of the Secret Intelligence Service. The man was tall and very effeminate. He always dressed to the nines, as if he were expecting to be greeted by the queen. But he was very good at his job, very good indeed. Under his tutelage, the SIS had grown and prospered into one of the most respected secret services in the world.

The driver left Briggs off at the front of the house, then continued around to the back.

"Good afternoon Donald," Sir Roger said, as Briggs mounted the steps.

"Hello, Sir Roger," Briggs said, shaking hands with the old man.

"Trust you had a good flight over?"

"Yes, sir," Briggs said. He turned to Hope-Turner, who managed a pinched smile as they shook hands.

"Hope we didn't inconvenience you too badly, O'Meara," the SIS chief said. His voice was soft, reedy. It belied his reputation for being a hard man.

"I was told this was to be a vacation, nothing more," Briggs said with an Irish lilt. He had learned Hope-Turner was having troubles with the Irish Republican Army of late.

Sir Roger chuckled. "Sylvia says you are incorrigible. I believe it."

"I saw her on the hill."

"Yes, she's working with the two-year-olds. Been at it since before eight," Sir Roger said. He led the way through the house to the table outside on the patio.

The cook had fixed them a light lunch of sliced meats and cheeses, cut fruit, and a good British ale. Briggs had forgotten how enjoyable this sort of food was, and he dug in hungrily.

"You haven't been up to much since that Soviet pipeline thing, have you?" Hope-Turner asked near the end of their lunch.

Briggs looked up and shook his head.

"From what I understand, it was quite a spectacular show."

Brigg's eyes narrowed. "Are you trying to goad me, sir?"

Hope-Turner looked surprised. "Heavens, no. Whatever gave you that idea?"

Briggs turned to Sir Roger. "Rudy asked that I come over. You had a favor to ask. Something he said was quite minor that needed taking care of. I agreed. But I did not agree to this sort of thing."

Before Sir Roger had a chance to reply, Hope-Turner jumped in.

"I'm frightfully sorry, old boy. Really I am," he said. "It's just that at the moment I've got my hands full with . . . Well, you began with that Irish bit of yours and I'm afraid it set me off. Sorry." He held out his hand.

"Sure," Briggs said. They shook hands. "Now, what's this about a job?"

"I brought you out here for purely selfish reasons, Donald. I wanted to see you. It's Stuart who has the job for you."

"I'm glad to be here, sir. How have you been?"

"Just fine. We've just come from Hong Kong, you know."

"Racing horses?"

"Yes. Calming the natives, what with this China thing hanging over everyone's head."

"And Sylvia?"

"She came along," Sir Roger said. He glanced over toward the paddocks. "She was supposed to have been up for lunch. She must have gotten carried away."

Briggs turned back to Hope-Turner. "I was told I

had the right of refusal."

"Of course. But I don't think you'll turn this down. It'll be a piece of cake. A little fun in the sun."

"I see."

"Yes, well. Have you heard of the Caroline Islands?"

"Of course. Micronesia. Just north of New Guinea, east of the Philippines."

"The very ones. We're building a satellite monitoring station out there. Or at least we've been trying for the past nine months or so."

"Weather satellite, spy satellite, what?" Briggs asked.

"A receiving station for the CIA's Eye-in-the-Sky system, actually. We've been invited to participate."

"But you are running into troubles? The natives? What?"

"Accidents. One week ago there was a terrible explosion in the fuel dump. Killed four workmen and severely burned eighteen others, at least three of whom are not expected to live."

"How'd it happen?"

"No one is sure. Just as they haven't been sure with the other mishaps. A boat sank, a tower collapsed, two fires, and one other explosion. All frightful."

"Someone is behind it? Maybe it's the Russians."

"Someone is behind it. The Chinese if anyone, though. This particular satellite is stationed over that part of the world."

"From what I understand, construction is way behind schedule, and the CIA is getting somewhat nervous with the delays," Sir Roger said.

"Very. They want to know if we are having a

problem we can't handle. If that's the case they'll pull back on their promise to let us use the system. A system which we need, Mr. O'Meara."

"Accidents can be prevented, sir. And if they're not accidents, we surely can pinpoint their source. It's either off the island, or on it."

"We have our man out there," Hope-Turner said. "Good chap. Steady hand. Name of Bob Graves."

"He's staying on the construction site?"

"Yes."

"Then of course he was spotted immediately."

"Yes," Hope-Turner said dryly. "We rather thought he would be. Hoped that would slow down whoever was working against us."

"It hasn't?"

"On the contrary, the situation has gotten worse out there."

"Graves have any ideas?"

"He thinks it's the work of the local copra baron there, a chap named Soshi Taranaga."

The name was very familiar to Briggs. "Any connection with the Japanese electronics firm?"

"He owns it."

"My God, the man must be a billionaire. What the hell is he doing making copra on a Pacific island?"

"He doesn't live there full time, of course," Hope-Turner said. "It's his little retreat. From the hustle-bustle of the business world. Every now and then he flies out from Tokyo to spend a couple of days, or sometimes as much as a week."

"Graves thinks Taranaga may be behind the accidents?" Briggs said, trying to digest what Hope-Turner was telling him. "But why? What motive would he have?"

"We don't know, except that Graves seems to think Taranaga hates westerners."

"I see," Briggs said. He finished his ale. "What did he do during the war? Was his family in Hiroshima or Nagasaki?"

"A soldier. A lieutenant, I believe. In fact, he was stationed on Truk for a time. Presumably he discovered his island during that time, and kept coming back. But we're not actually sure about all of that."

"Why's that?"

"Taranaga is rich. He's used his money to erase some of his past."

"What?"

Hope-Turner shrugged. "He was asked why, a few years ago, by a western journalist. Taranaga said, very straightforwardly, that his past was no one's business but his own."

"With that kind of money he can get away with it," Briggs said. He looked at Sir Roger. "If I had that dough, I might do a little switching of my own past."

Sir Roger and Hope-Turner both laughed at the little joke.

"What's to be done, then?" Briggs asked.

"That's just it—we want to know what's going on out there. Graves suspects Taranaga may have a hand in it, but he'll never be able to find out for sure, as exposed as he is."

"You want me in there—as an engineer replacing one of the ones just killed?"

"Exactly," Hope-Turner said. "There'd be an element of danger, of course. But it wouldn't exactly be like popping into Moscow to do some mischief."

"People have been getting killed on your little island, though, haven't they?"

Hope-Turner nodded.

"It's terribly important to us, Donald," Sir Roger said.

"Yes, sir," Briggs said. He got up and went to the serving cart. The lower shelf held an ice bucket, some liquor, and several bottles of the ale. He opened one of the ales, then took it to the edge of the patio and looked out across the back paddock.

He supposed it wasn't the assignments they passed his way that bothered him, it was the way in which they tried to bullshit him into accepting.

So this receiving station was important to British interests. He could understand that. So why hadn't Hope-Turner initiated a request, through channels, that would have gone across the pond, ending up on Rudyard Howard's desk?

Briggs had to smile at his own logic — or, illogic. They hadn't done that because they knew that the assignment would have either gotten lost in the bureaucratic shuffle, or that when it came right down to it, Briggs would have refused.

So, Sir Roger Hume had been called in. Jog Howard, Howard jogs Briggs, Briggs meets with Sir Roger, and the circle was complete.

Sylvia, riding a lovely chestnut, came around from the front. Briggs smiled, and turned away.

"All right," he said to Hope-Turner. "I'll go out there and have a look-see."

"Jolly good," the SIS chief said, getting to his feet and coming across to where Briggs stood.

"I don't know if I'll be able to do as much good as

you evidently think I will. But I'll try."

Hope-Turner looked into his eyes. "That's all we can ask, Briggs. It's all we can ask."

Briggs's gaze had gone past the SIS chief to Sir Roger, who was smiling and getting to his feet.

"Sure, sure," Briggs said, turning as Sylvia walked up.

"Oh, hello, Donald," she said, coolly pleasant. "I didn't know you had arrived yet."

"Hello Sylvia," he said. They shook hands, and then she nodded at Hope-Turner (who had always loved her), and went to her father. She kissed him on the cheek.

"You're late."

"Sorry, father," she said. "I forgot myself."

Sir Roger looked across to where Briggs was standing. "But you knew Donald was coming from America. You knew he would be here for lunch."

Briggs had to laugh out loud. At the moment he loved Sir Roger. The old man was great.

Sylvia turned, somewhat red-faced but still composed. Briggs had to hand it to her, she did have style. "Oh, I'm sorry," she said. "It must have slipped my mind."

Briggs's bag had been brought from his hotel. It had been agreed that he would stay with Sir Roger overnight. In the morning he would be collected, and taken up to the SIS training facility just outside Warwick.

"We'll need you for a day—at the most, two," Hope-Turner had said. "Brief you on the facts, a few of the speculations, and, of course, your field work, and then you can be off. We'll get you down to Darwin, and from there to Port Moresby. After that, it's a light plane ride over."

Later in the afternoon, before dinner, Briggs had gone out riding, alone, stopping high above the highway that led back to London.

He thought then for a bit about his youth in London with Oumi and the others. And he thought about his life in the States.

There had been a time there in Montana, just before he had run to Hollywood, when he had seriously thought about marriage.

In a way (only in a way, he would admit to himself) he had felt just a slight sense of family—of home, of belonging—of something greater than himself and the problem at hand.

For just a moment he had contemplated settling down. But the intellectual portion of his mind had realized that had he actually married the poor girl, she would have been doomed to a very unhappy life.

Briggs had wanderlust. Or, more accurately, he had a lust for the sense of adventure you got when you struck back against something or someone who had done you great harm.

A vendetta, Oumi had told him once. "We're all men and women with this very terrible vendetta. We will die with it. We will never give it up until we have our homeland."

Briggs had Oumi's vendetta. But he did not have even the dimmest hope of a homeland.

Dinner was coolly cordial, although Briggs could see that Sir Roger was somewhat upset with the way in which his daughter was behaving.

At first he had disapproved of any relationship that might develop between his daughter and Briggs. At this moment, however, he seemed unhappy that such a relationship was not developing.

Fortunately, for his heart, he did not know the extent to which their relationship had already grown, and then faltered.

Afterward, Sir Roger and Briggs went outside, where they walked along one of the bridle paths, talking about the assignment, about Hope-Turner whom Sir Roger respected but did not like, and about British colonialism.

Then it was time for bed. Sylvia was nowhere to be found, so Briggs said his good-nights, went upstairs where he took a bath, then crawled into bed, the sheets pleasantly cool against his nude body.

The window was open, and he could hear the night sounds. For a long time he lay there, thinking mostly about Sylvia. About the last time he had come back here, and Sir Roger had been gone. They had made love for three days straight, getting out of bed only when hunger or nature called.

In the end it had not been happy. Sylvia had wanted a commitment from him. But it was a commitment he simply could not give to her.

He loved her too much.

Of course he could not tell her that. She would never give up then. So it had to turn out this way. And laying there in bed, he chided himself for being disappointed that Sylvia had greeted him the way she had.

His bedroom door opened, and in the pale moonlight he could see that it was Sylvia. She came in, and closed the door. For a minute she stood there, looking across at him. She was dressed in a long, very thin nightgown, and nothing more.

Briggs slowly raised his left arm and looked at his watch. It was just before midnight.

"Were you expecting me?" Sylvia asked softly.

"No," Briggs said.

"I—" she started, but he cut her off.

"I wasn't expecting you, but I hoped you would come, darling."

He threw back the covers, and she came to him.

Three

Soshi Taranaga surveyed his domain from the window of the Bell Hc-1 helicopter. It was good to be back to the island. Tokyo had been bad enough, but for the past four months he had been spending a lot of time in New York City. His intended purchase of a Wall Street bank was being blocked by a number of influential western senators and congressmen. Getting them to see things his way had been a protracted affair.

He had won in the end, of course. He always did. Having a fortune of more than two billion dollars at his command was a powerful weapon indeed.

He smiled with the thought of the battle he had just won. One of the senators was dead—a suicide. One congressman had resigned, and would probably go to jail for accepting bribes. The actions would never be traced back to Taranaga or any of his subsidiaries, of course, but the damage was done. One of the senators would be soon getting a divorce, and two others would not be reelected.

In the end, he had been granted his purchase through intermediaries. The America public was not ready to be owned by a Japanese gentleman. Not yet. But the time would come when the Americans would pay dearly for everything they had done to his people. Their stinking ways, their abominable manners, their crude behavior would be held up for the world to look at, and ridicule.

The Americans and their British cousins were having their days in the sun. But that would change. There would come a time, very soon, when westerners would not even be allowed to lick the boots of their Japanese masters.

Just the thought of it brought shivers of anticipation to Taranaga.

It was called Swanson Island, and it was just north of the Namonuito Atoll near Truk Island. Behind him was the single small town, named after the missionary, Swanson, who'd founded the place, and ahead was the single volcanic mountain rising to the northeastern cliffs.

Taranaga's compound covered the entire eastern side of the island, and included the volcano itself, in whose high hills were the caves.

The British satellite receiving station was on the northern point, between the town and Taranaga's domain.

They said the station was for the reception of satellite weather data, but Taranaga knew differently. The American CIA had invited the British to liaise. His own intelligence sources were highly enough placed in Washington and London to discover that.

His spies also told him that the British would not take the accidents lying down. Despite Graves's puny efforts, they would almost certainly be sending someone else soon. They would have to.

Taranaga's people told him that the CIA was getting impatient. If the British did not straighten out their problems here on the island, the CIA would withdraw their offer to share data from the Spy-in-the-Sky system.

It would hurt their relationship, and the stupid Americans did not stop to realize that it was to their benefit to make sure the British were strong partners.

Westerners were so incredibly stupid, Taranaga thought. So incredibly stupid.

Along the southern shore was the copra processing plant, which until the beginning of construction of the receiving station provided the only employment on the U.S. Trust island.

Even the ownership of the island was a joke on the Americans. The entire area was a U.S. Trust. But on most of the islands, the natives and the Japanese who lived there hated Americans.

The helicopter began climbing over the ridges that led eventually to the slopes of the volcano still in the distance, and Taranaga could see his compound.

A large area had been cleared, and on it had been built many buildings, including the single large, rambling, Japanese-styled home, which was Taranaga's personal domain.

There were generator sheds, the barracks and huts for the native workmen, a small but well-equipped dispensary, and even a library with books and records in four different languages: Japanese, English, French, and a few translations in the strange, pidgin Polynesian tongue used by the natives in these parts.

In Tokyo, as well as in New York, Bern, Switzerland, Hong Kong, and a dozen other world capitals, Taranaga had to be careful. He had to maintain a front so that the financial wizards with whom he had to deal on a daily basis would not become nervous.

But here he was in a world of his choosing. Here there was only one rule — Taranaga's word. Here was a feudal system of farmers, and servants, and workmen, who owed their entire existence to their Japanese shogun.

The helicopter pilot skillfully brought the machine down for a landing just below the main house, and the staff — all Japanese — came out and lined up to greet him.

His secretary, Gloria Conley, an American whose Japanese was as good as could be expected from any westerner, also came down from the house.

She was tall, light of hair, with pale-blue eyes and lovely long legs. Taranaga owned her father, whom he had saved from a certain prison sentence after a Securities and Exchange Commission investigation had begun to turn up some irregularities in his business.

Taranaga had dealt with the little man on more than one occasion, as the American had supplied certain subassemblies in the U.S. for Taranaga Electronics.

He had had absolutely no feeling for Herbert Conley other than a low form of contempt, but his daughter, about to marry, was another story. She was intriguing.

It had taken nearly a month before the husband-to-be had been discredited, and was in jail, and before the father had convinced Gloria that their only salvation would be for them to go along with Taranaga.

At first she had resisted, of course. Taranaga had not minded that little show of spirit too badly. He had explained the facts of life to her, including what would probably happen to her father if he were sent to prison, since the old man had a heart condition . . .

Afterwards she had agreed to come to work for him, and do whatever — *whatever* — Taranaga asked of her, in exchange for her father's freedom.

Sooner or later the man would die, of course, and then the girl would be gone. But by then it would not matter. By then he would almost certainly be tired of playing with her.

Taranaga slid open the helicopter door, and stepped out as the rotor blades began to slow to a halt. His house staff all bowed respectfully, and he returned the gesture as a measure of affection for their loyalty.

But Gloria, her contempt for him barely concealed, merely smiled. "Welcome home, Taranaga-san," she said.

Taranaga strode across from the helicopter to where she stood. Without warning he backhanded her across her face, sending her reeling, her hand going to her mouth as blood trickled from her lip.

"You miserable western slut," he screamed. "You do not deserve to stand in the same line with these sincere, good people of impeccable manners."

"I am sorry, sir," Gloria said. She was shaking.

Taranga's house staff had lowered their eyes out of respect for the girl's shame. It made his heart swell with pride for them, while at the same moment his anger for Gloria—for the western values she represented—rose in his chest.

"Go to my quarters immediately," he screamed at her.

"Yes, Taranaga-san," she said, clasping her hands and bowing, finally. She turned, and scurried across the yard and into the house.

Taranaga's island manager, Nakasuri Ogi, stepped forward and bowed low. "Hai," he said.

Taranaga returned the bow. "You have done well. We will speak now."

Ogi bowed again, and then he turned and hurried up to the house, where he disappeared around the corner into Taranaga's office.

"There will be much work to be done, now," he addressed the rest of his house staff. "Soon there will be many people here. Some of them will mean us harm. We will have to be ever watchful."

They all bowed low. Taranaga returned it, then

went up to the house, a slight smile of anticipation on his lips.

Ogi was waiting in the compound office when Taranaga came in. The room was the only one in the house that made any concessions to western values.

Here were desk, file cabinets, bookcases, and a large map table. On the walls were photographs of the gigantic Taranaga Electronics factories around the world. There were also photographs of Taranaga shaking hands with a dozen different world leaders. He was not proud of his room, nor was he ever comfortable here. But the room was functional. It served to constantly reinforce his hatred of all things western.

He poured them both saki from the warmer. They toasted and drank. He poured another, and they sat.

"You have done well, my friend," Taranaga began. "This time, from what I am told, there were many deaths, many injuries, with absolutely no clue as to how the accident occurred."

"It was an electrical spark from a faulty generator—" Ogi began, but Taranaga gently interrupted him.

"The details are meaningless, Ogi. What is important are results. The British are on the run. They are frightened that they will lose their contract. But even more importantly, the Americans are vexed. They are rapidly losing confidence in their British friends."

Taranaga rubbed his hands together. This was going very well. Very well indeed.

"Then it will not be long before the British leave?" Ogi asked.

"They will try one last time to discover if I am behind their troubles. They do not want to believe it is so, because of my power in western circles. They fear and respect my wealth and power. Why would someone such as myself bother with an insignificant receiving station?"

"Perhaps they believe it is the Chinese."

"We do not want them to believe that!" Taranaga was quick to shout. "We do not want that. We want them to believe it is me, without being able to do a thing about it! That is of supreme importance! The pitiful fools must be made to squirm like a firefly on a killing needle, their light slowly extinguished in exquisite pain."

Ogi sat perfectly still, his eyes straight to the front. Taranaga was a very dangerous man when he worked himself into this state.

Taranaga calmed down, though. "The British will almost surely send someone to make sure. He will be their best. But we will be better."

"Yes," Ogi said, still not daring to move.

Taranaga drained his saki cup, slammed it down, and went to the door. "I will not be disturbed for twenty-four hours, Ogi. See to it."

Ogi jumped up, and bowed deeply. "Yes, Taranaga-san."

The huge house was laid out in several wings that radiated from the central core, which included a lovely rock garden.

Taranaga's private wing was far off to the north, and encompassed its own rock garden, complete with small pools, running water, and a lovely, large veranda.

Only a handful of people had ever seen this garden, which Taranaga had built himself with his own two hands in the ancient traditions.

Gloria Conley waited for him on the veranda, just outside the bathhouse. She had changed, and was now wearing a spotlessly white kimono, no shoes on her feet, her blond hair pinned up in the back.

She lowered her head when he came to her.

"I am sorry if I have offended you—" she began.

Taranaga hit her a powerful blow on the side of her head. She fell to the side, tumbling off the veranda.

"I will take my bath now," he said imperiously, and he stalked into the bathhouse, where he spread his arms and waited.

A moment or two later, Gloria came in and slipped his robe off, hung it on a hook, and then came back and undid his loincloth, laying it aside.

He lifted one foot at a time, and she took off his stockings and sandals, laying them aside as well.

On a small raised platform, Taranaga took a shower, Gloria, now nude as well, helping him wash his back, his arms and legs, and even his genitals.

When she was finished, he stepped down, slapped her across the face, then spun her around and slapped her four times very hard across the buttocks, leaving his handprints in red.

He laughed as he stepped into the steaming hot water, and eased himself down. A water lily floated just inches from his face. He focused on it, but then looked up as Gloria came into the bath with him.

For the next hour, Taranaga gave himself over to Gloria's ministrations, to her massages, to her caresses.

From time to time he would slap her face, or order her half out of the huge circular tub so that he could look at her body, and slap her legs or her buttocks.

Then she would climb back in the tub, tears leaking from her eyes, to continue bathing him.

Her shame, so absolute, was so wonderful that at times it was hard for Taranaga to bear. At times he thought that he would surely burst.

"You are nothing but the dung of a dog," he said softly.

"I am nothing but the dung of a dog, Taranaga-san," Gloria repeated.

"Your father is shit."

"My father is shit."

"You are an eater of shit."

"I am an eater of shit."

Taranaga laughed, his enjoyment of the humor immense. He spread his legs, then grabbed her head and shoved it underwater. She came to him without fight, taking him in her mouth, and frantically moving back and forth. It was up to her to make sure he came before she drowned.

It was barely 9:00 **a.m** when the jeep bounced up the back country lane, stopping at the tall gate in the wire-mesh fence. A big sign said: WARNING, RESTRICTED GOVERNMENT AREA, ACCESS FORBIDDEN.

Briggs's driver, a taciturn young man with pimples, handed over his pass to the guard who had materialized out of a small hut, then signed in on a clipboard.

The gate swung open, and they went through; a half mile farther on they came to a rambling stone house beside a lovely stream. The driver pulled up.

"This is it, guv'. End of the line."

"Thanks for the lift," Briggs said. He got out, and grabbed his bag from the back. He looked at the kid, shook his head, and grinned. "Anyone ever tell you that you talk too much?"

The kid laughed. "All the time," he said. He swung the jeep around on the road, and headed back the way they had come.

In a minute, the sound of the jeep's engine was lost. It was a lovely day. The sound of the brook running over stones, the birds singing, and the occasional breeze through the thick foliage were all pleasant.

"It's sorta restful, ain't it," someone said behind him.

Briggs turned around. An old woman stood in the doorway of the stone house. She was smiling.

"This is it?" he asked. "This is the training base?"

"The house is a lot bigger than it looks. Of course, you could just stay out there all day."

Briggs walked up the path. She took his bag. "Name's Katy," she said. "They say I have a photographic memory, so they don't have to stock a big library out here when it comes time for a briefing. They just send me down."

"Is that so," Briggs said.

"Yup. But I think the real reason is that I don't put up with any bullshit, so's we get our training down pat first time out. Catch my drift?"

Briggs laughed. "No, but I expect I will before too long."

"I expect you will," Katy said.

It was very late when Taranaga emerged from his sleeping quarters and lit a cigarette, sitting nude in the middle of his veranda as he contemplated the peace of his rock garden.

But there was much on his mind. Besides the wonders of Gloria's body, and the lengths to which she would degrade herself, he had to constantly be aware of his business. Running such a vast empire as his was a full-time job in itself. Combined, as it was, with a vendetta against all things western, the task was herculean.

But for now, he could listen to the sounds of the running water, pleasant now, the very soft, warm breezes caressing his skin that had been soaked with sweat.

For a time he could contemplate the honest, pure effort that had gone into this garden. The old tradition would not allow a single rock to be placed in anger.

Each moment that he had worked on his refuge, he had been at peace with himself, and with the world. At times, the long task had been made longer because he could not bring that inner peace to himself, and he had made himself stay very far away, so as not to contaminate this place.

Like much of his life, this too was a contradiction, of course, because just a few feet away, lying in her own blood and sweat, was Gloria Conley, a symbol of his hatred for the west.

But for the moment, he didn't want to think of that. He wanted to keep his mind clear. He was girding for the upcoming fight.

A jungle bird shrieked its raucous call far off in the direction of the volcano. Taranaga turned that way. He could see the bulk of the mountain rising up over the walls of his garden.

"Up there," he whispered to himself. Up there in the caves, and away in a hillside grave were the secrets. Up there was the generator that ran his life. The motive force of his hatred. Up there stretching back so many years.

Wasted . . . futile years?

He clamped those thoughts off, forcing his mind back to peace. To calmness. To his garden. But something else began to intrude. Something nagging, something frightening.

He raised his head, testing the air with his nose, as if he could sniff out his demons.

There was one coming from the west. One whose life force was very strong. Taranaga could almost feel the magnetism from this distance.

Of course, his feeling was nothing more than a strong intuitive grasp of the fact that the British would have to send someone.

Yet he could almost see the man. Tall. Very strong, but with a weakness about him. Something from his past would make him vulnerable.

Taranaga closed his eyes. With his other senses, he could see his rock garden and the small pools of water more clearly.

There would be a fight. But it would be a fight for the past. Taranaga's versus the man's coming.

Four

They watched the cloud formation on the horizon until they were close enough to see that an island was set beneath it in the perfectly blue ocean.

The trip out had been much easier than Briggs had supposed it would be. A 747 to Australia, a twin jet to Port Moresby in New Guinea, and finally a DeHavilland out to the islands.

But Briggs was worried. He had been ever since Darwin, when two Japanese men had joined the flight. He had not bothered with introductions, and they had seemed content to remain by themselves. But Briggs had begun to get the over-the-shoulder feeling that he often did when he was being watched.

These two were watching him. He'd be willing to bet almost anything on it.

During the long flight up over the big island of New Guinea, and then across the ocean, Briggs had tried to work it out.

On the assumption that Taranaga was indeed hampering the British work—never mind for the moment the man's reasons—he was rich enough to field his own intelligence-gathering network. But rich enough, Briggs wondered, to penetrate the U.S. State Department, or the British Secret Intelligence Service?

Probably. So it could very well mean that Taranaga knew someone was being sent out to investigate the accidents.

Another possible explanation, however, was that Taranaga merely assumed that someone would be coming. He was a smart man, and it was a reasonable assumption. The British could not take this lying down.

Taranaga—assuming still that the Japanese billionaire was behind the accidents—would expect that the British would be sending their man disguised. Most likely as a replacement engineer for the ones who had recently been killed.

That's what Taranaga would be expecting. That's what Hope-Turner had set up for him. And that's what the big woman, Katy, had done for him. She had taught him the short course on electronics engineering, especially as it applied to high-frequency satellite data tracking, acquisition, and reception.

But Katy had also reinforced something he had always known, something that his émigré mentors had drummed into his head since he was a lad.

After dinner one night, he had been taking a stroll with Katy.

"Of course all this could turn out to be rubbish, pure and simple balderdash," Katy had said without preamble.

In their very short time together Briggs had come to have an affection, and a very deep respect for her. She was older—probably in her late fifties or early sixties—she was grossly overweight, and she wasn't particularly good looking, but she was a beauty in Briggs's eyes. She was bright, sharp as a tack, and had a memory that was impossible to comprehend. "Ask me," she'd said once, "and I'll recite the bloody Britannica for you." He believed it.

"What do you mean by that?" Briggs had asked.

She stopped and looked directly into his eyes. "Look, my boy. Hope-Turner is a dandy fellow and all that. Very smart cookie, he is. Runs the service with iron mitts, not the pastel gloves you might expect, but he's gone a bit rigid on this one. Convinced it can't be Taranaga. The Japper is just too big a fish, if you get my drift."

Briggs nodded, although he hadn't caught her drift yet.

"But look here, let's assume it is Taranaga-san after all, luv. Let's say the Nip is off his bat. Dipping into the juice, or some such. He's a powerful cookie, he is. He'll figure you out in a flash, so you had best be ready and able to jump whichever way the daggers fly. Now do you catch my drift?"

Briggs had. "With all due respect to Hope-Turner, I had planned a couple of things on my own. Pays to have a back door to slip out. In fact I'm—"

Katy cut him short. "No, luv," she'd said, giving him a hug. "I don't want to hear it. Cause if I do, and if Hope-Turner asks me, I'll have to tell him the truth. I think your plans are your own."

Taranaga was expecting an engineer. If the two

men who had joined the flight in Darwin were working for him, they were in for a big surprise.

Briggs reached down under his seat, opened his carry-on case, and pulled out the Gideon Bible he had stolen from his Port Moresby hotel.

He looked out the window. They would soon be making their approach for landing.

He stood up. "Ladies and gentlemen, if I could just have your attention."

There were eight people aboard. The door to the flight deck was open, and the pilot and copilot turned around to see what their passengers were doing. The two Japanese were watching Briggs intently, their eyes wide.

"This has been a god-given flight to a wondrous land. Soon we will be touching down. In my exuberance, I merely wanted to offer my heartfelt blessings for a safe voyage."

He made a vague sign of the cross in the air, lowered his head, mumbled something, then raised his hands into the air, holding the bible up. "God bless us all!" he shouted in a tent-revival preacher's voice. He sat down.

For a long moment no one said a word, then one of the passengers tittered, and everyone else sat back to look out their windows. Except for the two Japanese who were staring toward Briggs.

Briggs nodded. "Bless you, brothers," he said. They were just across the aisle. He reached over and held out his hand. "Don't believe I caught your names. I'm Brother S. Rupert Blake, a journalist for

Canada For Christ magazine. Montreal."

The two Japanese looked at him for a long moment as if he was some sort of oddity, then they turned away.

Briggs grinned. "Bless you," he said, and then under his breath "—you sonofabitches."

They landed at the airstrip outside the town of Swanson about noon, and even before the plane's doors were opened Briggs knew it would be hot.

The island was only a few degrees above the equator, and although there usually was an ocean breeze, especially at night and very early in the morning, midday was always like a blast furnace.

This day was no exception. Within seconds of the time he stepped off the aircraft, Briggs's clothes were plastered to his body. The sun was like a blowtorch directly overhead.

He and the other passengers straggled across the field to the small customs shed. The copilot caught up with him when he was nearly there.

"I wanted to thank you for your kind words, padre," the man said.

Briggs smiled. "Well, bless you, my son, but I'm not a padre. I'm just a simple journalist."

They continued walking and entered the hot, airless, fly-infested shed where the others were beginning to go through the customs routine.

"What brings you to this part of the world, then?" the copilot asked. He was British. A hard-bitten sort, but with friendly, honest eyes. Briggs wondered if Hope-Turner hadn't sent him tagging along to keep tabs on the American free-lancer.

Briggs turned to look at the other passengers, especially the two Japanese who were seemingly paying no attention to the exchange.

"I've come here to do a story on the Godless Japanese gentleman who has inhabited this island since the war," Briggs said loudly. "Taranaga, I believe, is the gentleman's name."

The copilot nearly lost it. He grinned. "I see," he said, and he turned and went back out to the plane, leaving Briggs standing there alone.

He was the last to be cleared through customs, and it was nearly an hour later before he was allowed to go. It was curious, he thought. This was American soil, the American flag flew over the customs shed, the customs officers wore American uniforms, but they were of Japanese extraction.

The island's only bus and two cabs were gone. The pilot and copilot had already gone into town, which was about two miles away, and as Briggs stood there looking down the dusty road, the two customs men, riding in a jeep, roared past him. Neither one of them looked back.

Briggs smiled, hoisted his bags and his jacket to his shoulder, and started into town. He had fired the opening shot into the bushes, not sure if anyone was in there. But the place had been alive with critters, all of them scurrying for cover now.

Halfway into town, Briggs had stopped to pull a hat from his suitcases, and when he walked into the relatively cool lobby of the Swanson Hotel, he felt as if he were a horse that had been ridden hard and put away wet. He was in no mood for any desk clerk to tell him that the obviously almost-empty hotel was full. Yet he understood that he would have to remain in character. Fortunately, the clerk was not Japanese; he was a short, fat Polynesian, with wide, rolling eyes.

"Sorry, sir, but we're all full up. No rooms today. Try again tomorrow."

Briggs stepped back, puffing himself up. He fumbled in his bag for his Bible. He held it opened, overhead, and began, in Russian, to chant the poem, "Jada's Theme," from *Dr. Zhivago*. Then he began to hop from one foot to the other, as he turned slowly around.

The desk clerk's eyes were nearly bulging out of his head. He was licking his lips and his breath was coming in short gasps.

Briggs raised his voice, and danced even harder.

The clerk held out his hands as if to ward off the evil spirits that he was certain Briggs was conjuring. "no . . . please, no," he cried.

Briggs chanted even more loudly, hopping higher and higher as he spun around. A number of people hearing the commotion had come in from the street to watch the crazy Canadian preacher man. His reputation was already beginning to spread.

"No!" the clerk screamed.

Briggs stopped, and pointed his finger at the frightened desk clerk. "Death to you and your family if you have lied to me! If you have blasphemed my God!"

"No! No!" the clerk squealed. He brought the

registration book up from under the counter and held it out. "Here," he cried. "There are rooms. There is a room for you. Here, please."

Briggs grinned hugely. He put his Bible away, stepped up to the desk, and signed the register with a flourish. "S. Rupert Blake," he said. "*Canada For Christ* magazine. I will be here for at least a fortnight."

He hefted his bags, and the clerk handed him a key. "Second floor, front."

There wasn't a bellman, so Briggs went up by himself. The room was larger than he thought it would be, with a large fan in the middle of the ceiling, typhoon shutters open to catch a stray breeze, the large bed in the center of the room draped with mosquito netting.

Briggs hung up his clothes, changed into khakis, his stiletto beneath his shirt at the small of his back, hid his spare money and passports in the motor unit of the overhead fan, then poured himself a stiff Irish whiskey from the bottle he had brought with him.

At the window, he leaned against the wall and looked down at the main street of the town. It was paved. Aside from the single highway that ran the length of the island, it was the only paved road here. Everything else was dirt — mud in the rainy season.

There had been copra processing going on here for a very long time — long before the memory of anyone here. Official French records showed that plantation operations had been going on since the early eighteen-hundreds with no stops — not even for the war.

The inhabitants were a mix mostly of French and Polynesian, or at least had been until just before the Second World War, when the Japanese had taken over. The island had not been the same since.

Across the street was a block-long row of shops, with apartments on the second floor. Beyond was a wide park, and beyond that the public docks in the harbor.

Behind the hotel was the shipping company's storage yard, where everything from lumber to liquor was stored; to the south was the generator plant where electricity for the town was produced. The copra plant had its own generator, as did the satellite receiving station and Taranaga's compound in the foothills on the opposite end of the island.

Behind the shipping yard were several blocks of hovels where the natives lived, and beyond that was uninterrupted jungle all the way to the north shore.

This island had been a Japanese stronghold during the war, but one that the Allies had never bothered to hit. It had not been strategic enough.

Briggs was reasonably certain that Taranaga had chosen this island as his personal Shangri-la because of the war. Evidently, as a young man he had been stationed here on the island, or nearby, and had been impressed.

He thought it was possible that Taranaga sought the removal of the British station for no other reason than he wanted this island for himself. He did not want his paradise sullied.

One of the Japanese men who had gotten on the

plane in Darwin came around the corner and went into the restaurant across the street. Briggs smiled. Bingo! They had been sent to watch out for whoever the Brits might be sending.

Briggs finished his drink, then left the room. Instead of going down the front stairs to the lobby, however, he went to the other end of the corridor, opened the window, and looked outside.

Below was a foul-smelling drainage ditch filled with every imaginable kind of junk, from lumber and wooden crates to a doll carriage and a rusting hunk of corrugated iron.

Briggs quickly slipped out the window, hung on the ledge by his fingertips, and let go, dropping the ten or twelve feet onto the soft earth.

He got up, brushed himself off, and hurried along the backs of the buildings to the end of the row, then stepped around the corner and crossed the street to the rear of the building across from the hotel.

At length he came to the rear of the restaurant. A Japanese man was just emptying the garbage into a pigsty that contained a huge sow and half a dozen piglets.

He stopped when he saw Briggs.

"Hai! What you do here?"

Briggs held his finger to his lips. Then he made a sign of the cross over the man, and handed him a five-dollar bill. The sign did not impress him; the money did.

"What do you want back here, preacher?" the Japanese said.

"I want to use your back door, and I don't want

all your cousins knowing about it," Briggs said.

"Oh . . . Sure, go ahead," the man said.

"I wouldn't want to have to return for my money."

"Sure, go ahead. No sweat."

Briggs nodded, and entered the restaurant. He passed quickly through the kitchen, stepped out into the restaurant itself, and walked up to where the Japanese man who had been following him since Darwin was seated, watching the front of the hotel.

"Why, it's a fellow traveler. Hello there," Briggs said.

The man jumped nearly out of his skin when he realized who it was. He glanced quickly toward the kitchen and then back up at Briggs.

"Cat got your tongue, brother?" Briggs asked. He bent down so that he could get the same line of sight as the man, and he looked up toward the second floor of the hotel. "Nice view," he said. He grinned.

"What do you want? Why are you following me?" the Japanese asked.

"Ah," Briggs said expansively. "You do know how to talk. But you have it wrong, friend. I am not following you. On the contrary, you are following me. Why? Don't you trust Canadian journalists here?"

The man said nothing.

Briggs nodded, then straightened up. "I see. There is little doubt in my mind that you work for Taranaga-san, the godless wretch who lives here. You may tell him that I have come to save his soul."

The Japanese man blinked, but said nothing. Hate radiated from him as a palpable force. It almost colored the air around the table.

Why, Briggs had to wonder. Why the strong emotion?

He stepped back, then left the restaurant and went back to the hotel. The same Polynesian clerk jumped up when Briggs approached the desk.

"I need a car," Briggs said.

"And a driver too, boss?"

"Just a car," Briggs said. "I'm going sightseeing."

"Ain't much here to see—" the clerk started to say, but he cut himself off. Briggs was one man he wasn't going to argue with. "Yes, sir," he said. He turned around, grabbed a set of keys on a bamboo ring, and handed them across. "It's my car," he said. "The good lookin' '65 Chevy out front. You may have to get some gas back at the depot. Tell 'em to put it on your bill here."

"Thanks," Briggs said, looking at the clerk. He decided to press just a little harder. "How do I get out to Soshi Taranaga's stronghold?"

The clerk nearly swallowed his tongue. He shook his head. "Oh no, boss, you don't want to go out there. It's definitely off limits."

"Right," Briggs said. "But how do I get out there?"

"Boss, if Taranaga-san finds out I sent you out there, he would certainly . . ."

"He would certainly what?" Briggs asked. But the clerk was staring past Briggs at the front door. Briggs turned around. The other Japanese man from the plane stood in the doorway. He grinned hugely.

"Ah, it is the Reverend Blake," he said, coming the rest of the way across the lobby. He held out his hand. Briggs shook it.

"Your friend is across the way in the restaurant," Briggs said.

"I know, I know. I just left him. Poor fellow. I came immediately over to apologize for his very rude behavior."

"Oh?"

"Yes. You see he had led a very sheltered life until now. He was until very recently a Shinto priest — or I should say he was studying for the discipline. Sadly, he discovered it was not for him. So, you see, you are not only a rare sight for him as a westerner in these parts, but you are a preacher of a totally alien religion."

"That's why he was following me?"

The man nodded. "Please. I am Nojima Tosu. I could not help but overhear that you wished to learn the road out to Taranaga-san's home.

"Yes."

"Permit me," he said. "On this island everything is very easy. You merely stay on the paved highway past the processing plant, and you will come to the Rising Sun. It is Taranaga-san's home."

"Thank you," Briggs said. "How, then, would I reach the British station that is under construction here."

"The very same highway," Tosu said, still grinning. "There is a turnoff to the north along the road. A large sign marks the place. You cannot miss it."

"Thanks again, brother," Briggs said.

"If I may make a suggestion, sir," Tosu said.

Briggs looked at him, but then nodded.

"Go see the base this afternoon. Tonight, or perhaps by tomorrow, Taranaga-san will most assuredly invite you to his home for tea, or perhaps even dinner. He often does that when strangers arrive here."

"He wants to know who is visiting his island and why?" Briggs asked.

"Indeed," Tosu said, bowing.

Five

The bright equatorial sun shone in thin stripes from the slats of the blinds covering the large windows in the low ceilinged room. It was relatively cool here, because of the thick jungle growth around the building, because of the heavy woven mat roof, and because of the long-bladed electric fans that swirled slowly overhead.

Ten slight-of-build men, dressed in black pajamas, with black cotton face and head coverings, their feet bare, marched silently into the room, single file.

They stopped at the front, aligning themselves into a semicircle, all facing the door they had just entered by.

An old man, obviously a priest by his actions, came into the room, knelt before a fire ring, and lit several large pieces of ceremonial — and slightly narcotic — incense.

When the faint curls of smoke began to rise, he

got up from the grass matting on the floor, faced the ten black-clad men, bowed, and then turned and left the room.

Not one of the men moved so much as a muscle, and they all would have remained in exactly that position, unless they were instructed to do otherwise, until they kneeled over dead. They were, in fact, disciplined to a fanatical degree.

From the room, the sounds of the surf crashing on the beach far to the north could be heard, as could the sounds of the jungle birds, and the wind rushing around the volcano peak upland. Here also could be heard the running water within the rock garden twenty yards away.

The door opened, and Soshi Taranaga, wearing the same black cotton pajamas, but without the mask, entered.

The ten black-clad ninja warriors bowed deeply. Taranaga returned the greeting once he was in position in front of them within the semicircle.

One of the ninja stepped forward, and bowed again. Taranaga returned the second greeting.

"There is a westerner who has recently arrived on our island. I believe he is the man the British call Donald O'Meara. However, he identifies himself now as a Canadian Christian magazine writer. But it is a subterfuge. I am certain of it," Taranaga said.

"Yes, master," the senior ninja said.

Taranaga studied his lieutenant for a long moment. "Death or dishonor," he said. "Each is yours. Each comes of your choice."

"Yes, master," his lieutenant said softly.

"This man was sent to kill me. He must die," Taranaga said dispassionately.

"He will die, master," the lieutenant said.

"He will die, master!" all ten ninja warriors repeated.

Taranaga bowed very low, as a sign of his extreme respect and confidence in his people, and then turned confidently away and left the room. However it would happen, whatever weapons or means they would use, he was certain that the man called O'Meara would soon be dead.

In the meantime there was breakfast, and then he would unleash his other weapon.

Briggs stopped the ancient, blue-smoking Chevy, set the parking brake, and got out. He was afraid to shut off the engine. It probably would not start again. There was nothing about the car that was not shot or sun-rotted.

He walked across the road, the asphalt nearly liquid under the intense sun, and looked up the road toward Taranaga's compound.

About five miles back he had passed the big sign that marked the turnoff to the British satellite receiving station, but he had continued on the highway. Out of curiosity, he supposed. Although he was fairly certain that Taranaga would invite him out, probably within the next twenty-four to forty-eight hours.

There was little to see from here, except for the roofs of a couple of buildings on the slopes of the volcano's foothills and a radio tower equipped with a small dish antenna for the transmission of telephone signals via satellite.

Briggs got back in the old Chevrolet, made a careful U-turn on the highway, and headed back to the turnoff.

There was going to be trouble here. A lot of it. He could feel it in the air. The entire island was thick with an atmosphere of death and mystery. Nearly everything here was out of the thirties and forties, except for the cars and a few other modern pieces of technology.

It was almost as if time had stopped, just before the war that had never reached here. It was, in a way, as if the island were still waiting for the Allied invasion that would never come.

A jeep came by from town, and Briggs clearly identified the cook from the Japanese restaurant through which he had come from the hotel. The man was so intent on his driving, however, that he never noticed Briggs.

It was starting already, he thought. There'd be a steady stream of informers from town out to Taranaga's compound. Every time Briggs moved, someone would be there to report on it.

He turned off the main road and headed out the dirt road through the jungle toward the north shore of the island, where the British satellite receiving station was being constructed.

This was a new road, heavily rutted from some of the heavy equipment that had been brought down here. When the rains came it would become totally impassable. By then, though, he supposed, it would have been filled in and finally paved.

It was only a few miles up to the north shore, and he came at length to a tall wire mesh fence, a large gate blocking the road.

Beyond were the large dishes being constructed, along with the buildings that housed, in air-conditioned comfort, the receiving equipment itself.

Hope-Turner had said this was to be a preliminary analysis station, as well. Which meant more extensive facilities would have to be constructed. There would at least have to be a primary computer center, and then the barracks, mess hall, and recreation center for the analysts and technicians.

Two armed guards, wearing British army drab, came out of the gatehouse as he slowed down and stopped.

He got out of the car as the guards came up.

"Good afternoon, sir," one of them said. "Something we can help you with?"

The other guard hung back. He was nervously fingering his automatic weapon. A lot of people had been killed here, so they were understandably jittery.

"I've come to see your station manager, a chap named John Bower," Briggs said.

"Is Mr. Bower expecting you, sir?"

"No, my sons, but if you will only tell him that S. Rupert Blake from *Canada for Christ* magazine is here, I'm sure he will see me."

"Bloody hell," the guard said. "Around with you, then; against the car, spread your legs."

Briggs did as he was told, and the guard frisked him, not coming up with Briggs's stiletto. He made note that he'd have to talk to Bob Graves, the SIS man about the efficiency of their people out here.

"Now, why don't you be a good little lad and run off," the guard said.

"I'll stay here all day and all night, if necessary, you boorish little man," Briggs said, puffing up.

"Right," the guard said dryly. He turned to the other guard. "Give Graves a call, then. Tell him what we've got out here."

"Sir," the other man said, and he hurried back to the gatehouse.

"Now, what sort of magazine did you say you was from, mate?"

"May your soul rot in hell for your blasphemy," Briggs said.

The guard laughed out loud. "You're too late with your curse, padre. This island is hell. So you see, I'm already there — body, soul and everything."

Briggs got back in the car, and Bob Graves, a short, stocky man with long wavy brown hair, showed up a few minutes later. He had been advised that Briggs was coming, but as an engineer, and under the name Donald O'Meara. He recovered nicely, however, when Briggs introduced himself as Blake.

"I see," Graves said. "Well, it's certainly a pleasure to see you here, Mr. Blake. I'm sure Mr. Bower, and John Webb — he's our construction supervisor — will be happy to see you."

"Wonderful," Briggs said, beaming.

Graves glanced distastefully at the old Chevy. "Why don't we leave your car here. We can ride up together in mine. The boys won't mind watching yours."

"That will be fine, just fine, brother," Briggs said.

He and Graves got in the SIS station-chief's jeep, and went through the gate and up the dirt road that continued through the jungle toward the installation under construction.

"Welcome to the Pacific, Mr. O'Meara," Graves began.

"Nope," Briggs said. "It's S. Rupert Blake. Don't forget it. I'm not your replacement engineer. I'm just a simple journalist from a Canadian religious magazine."

"Doing what here on the island? What's your cover?"

"I'm here to do an exposé on the godless wretch, Soshi Taranaga."

Graves's eyebrows rose, and he let out a low whistle. "Hope-Turner said you had balls."

Briggs grinned. "He tells me that you think all your troubles out here are because of Taranaga."

"Right, but it's a view not shared by Whitehall, I'm afraid."

"Anything concrete? Any motives?"

"Just a feeling, O'Meara ... er, Blake. Taranaga-san hates westerners and all things western."

"How do you know that?" Briggs asked. "I mean, the man has made his fortune from westerners and things western."

"Right. But the robber doesn't have to like his victim."

"I see," Briggs said.

They had come to the largest of the buildings, this one across the compound from the huge dish antennas under construction. The building was made of concrete block, and was air-conditioned.

When they stepped inside, the coolness seemed almost harsh after the intense heat and humidity.

A large, stocky man with thick, dark hair and a broad, sun-weathered face, wearing dirty khakis, came out of an office at the end of a short corridor. He came over when he spotted Graves.

"When are we getting that help you promised —" the man growled, stopping in mid-sentence as he realized that Graves had brought a stranger with him.

"John Webb — S. Rupert Blake, a Canadian journalist," Graves said.

Webb, who was the construction supervisor, had started to hold out his hand, but then he pulled it back. "A goddamned newspaper man?"

"No," Graves said. "It's not what you think," he added under his breath. He glanced beyond Webb down the hall. "Is Joseph in his office."

Webb nodded.

"Let's go down and talk to him."

"I've got too much to do this morning."

"You'll want to hear this, John," Graves insisted. "Believe me."

Webb finally acquiesced, and they all went into the station manager's outer office, past his startled secretary, and through to his inner office.

Joseph Bower was a tall, gray-haired gentleman who seemed as though he would have been more at home behind a leather-topped desk in some old established office, or in the board room of an important bank, than here in the middle of the jungle.

He rose from his desk. "Bob?" he said to Graves, as he looked at Briggs. "Is this our man?"

Graves waited until the door was closed, and then he nodded. "But he's not here as one of our engineers. I'll let him tell you all that, though."

Webb seemed relieved. "You mean you're not a newspaper man?"

"Nope," Briggs said. "But I am here to see what I can do to help."

"At last," Bower said.

They all sat down, and Briggs quickly went over his cover as S. Rupert Blake and what had happened to him already, including the two Japanese men who had begun tailing him in Darwin.

"I was worried about that," Graves said.

"What's that?" Briggs asked.

"Taranaga is very powerful . . . I mean, *very* powerful, in all the right circles in Washington, Paris, London. He's evidently got his people in or around the SIS, or perhaps with your own State Department in Washington. He knew someone would be coming out here."

"I thought the same thing," Briggs said. "If that's true, then he won't really be fooled by my new cover."

"He could be expecting nothing more than an engineer," Webb said.

"No," Briggs said. "The one who calls himself Nojima Tosu came over to the hotel just before I left today, and told me that Taranaga would most likely be inviting me out to his place."

"You won't go, of course," Bower said from behind his desk.

"Naturally I'll go," Briggs replied, smiling. "No matter what happens between now and the time I'm invited—and believe me, gentlemen, I think a lot will happen—I'll be at his house."

"But that would be suicide—if indeed the man is behind all of this," Bower protested. He turned to Graves for support. "Tell him, Bob."

"I'm afraid Mr. O'Meara is correct in this case, sir. We're going to get nowhere pussyfooting around."

"Right," Briggs said. "And now, I'd like to be shown around the site, if I may. But as an ordinary tourist, not as a new engineer; certainly not as an investigator."

They all got to their feet. "You can fit right in with the others," Webb said.

"The others?"

"Right," the construction supervisor said dourly.

Bower broke in. "From time to time we've invited a few of the townspeople and a few of the island administrators out to show them we're not building missile silos."

"Among them Taranaga's people," Briggs said.

"Right," Graves replied.

"Cozy."

Bower and Webb looked at each other. Bower came around his desk. "As long as you're here, will you be staying at the hotel in town?"

"Right," Briggs said. "Taranaga may guess who I am, but he cannot be absolutely sure. I don't

77

believe his people have been able to penetrate our security *that* deeply."

"Keep him on his toes," Graves said.

"And it'll keep Mr. O'Meara on his toes as well," Webb said.

Briggs looked at him.

"There'll be an accident for you, Mr. O'Meara, mark my words."

"I hope so," Briggs said. "I definitely hope so."

They all went outside, and between Bower and Webb Briggs was given the grand tour, which included the half-completed buildings, as well as the huge receiving dishes, and the communications antennas on the edge of the cliffs overlooking the ocean.

Already the afternoon breeze was beginning, so that although it was still terribly hot, there was some relief from it.

At least a hundred workmen, almost all of them imported from Australia, Canada, and England herself, were busy at work on the site. Huge cranes rose high into the equatorial sky. Bulldozers scraped; huge earthmovers carted load after load of dirt away. Construction crews raised buildings. High steel workers scrambled over and under the scaffolding around the dishes.

All in all it was a very impressive operation, with no sign that anything was amiss, until you came close enough to see the expression on the faces of the workmen.

They were all frightened. It was obvious from the way they looked, from the way they worked, from the way they constantly looked over their shoulders to see who or what was coming up behind them.

"There is a lot of superstition going on around here," Graves told Briggs at one point.

"How do you mean?"

"No matter what we say to the men, we can't come right out and tell them that someone is trying to sabotage the operation," Graves said.

"Hell, we'd have a mutiny on our hands," Webb said.

"So you tell them nothing?" Briggs asked.

"There's nothing we can tell them. So this project, for them, is jinxed."

"Right," Graves said.

They headed over to the main receiving antenna, which rose more than a hundred feet above the ground, spreading out like a gigantic saucer on a space-age cradle.

Two very large cranes moved large sections of the dish into place, while workmen on catwalks and a complicated latticework of scaffolding welded them in place.

"Big Bertha, we call this one," Webb said proudly.

"Like the World War Two cannon?" Briggs asked.

"One and the same, partner. We're shooting our big guns with this one. This little toy would be able to detect the emissions from a garage door opener as far out as the planet Jupiter. All we want, though, is a satellite in a geophysical orbit about twenty thousand miles out."

"Impressive," Briggs said. But these were the

kinds of things that Taranaga intimately understood. This was his sort of business . . . space-age electronic marvels. Who better than a knowledgeable man to sabotage an operation?

The dish antenna's base was constructed on a twenty-foot-tall rise, that had been bulldozed into place. Tall concrete retaining walls held the millions of yards of sand, rock, and dirt in place. The antenna itself had to be elevated well above the local terrain, Bower explained, so that extraneous signals would not be picked up.

"Someone shaving in one of the barracks could set the entire thing off if we didn't raise it above the buildings," Bower said.

They went around the side of the retaining wall and climbed up the stairs to the actual base of the antenna. Far overhead, one of the huge cranes on its tower was moving a big section of the dish face toward the edge to bring it into place.

Webb was explaining to Briggs and to Bower how concrete was injected into molds, then pressurized during the curing process so that the resulting cement was super-hard, able to withstand the tremendous pressures that would be placed on the base mounts during the typhoons that swept these islands from time to time.

The itchy feeling between Briggs's shoulder blades came an instant before workmen far above in the scaffolding began shouting.

Briggs looked up in time to see the huge section of the dish face falling toward them. He grabbed Webb's arm, and dragged him to the left, as he slammed into Graves and Bower, knocking them both off to the side, sending them rolling over the concrete retaining wall, and at least ten feet down to the piles of sand below.

Moments later, the tremendous pile of antenna smashed into the base exactly where they had been standing, the din of squealing, twisting metal so loud it blocked out everything.

Six

Briggs and Graves stepped off the elevator, high above the crumpled remains of the section of dish face, and walked out along the windy catwalk toward the control position of the huge construction crane.

Halfway across, Briggs stopped and turned back to Graves. This was one spot he was reasonably certain they could not be overheard.

"I knew there'd be an accident," Briggs said. "I wondered how long it would take them."

"You think Taranaga set this up?"

"Who else? His people were on the plane with me from Darwin. They knew I was here on the island. And I'm sure it was no secret that I was coming out here today."

"Then it proves it," Graves said, shouting over the wind. There were whitecaps on the water far below.

"Not yet," Briggs said. "But it gives me a direction." He turned and continued along the catwalk, and entered the small control shack.

The crane operator, a burly New Zealander, lay forward over the controls, his head down, his arms crumpled beneath him.

He had fallen forward, and had shoved the cable release, sending the dish face plummeting.

Briggs stepped across to the man, and carefully lifted him up. There was a small, blue hole in the side of his head, just above his right ear.

Briggs looked out in that direction. The control house windows were open that way, facing toward the jungle to the east—toward Taranaga's compound.

Someone had hidden down in the jungle with a high-powered rifle. When the time was right they had fired.

But the accuracy required had been incredible. Almost too incredible. . . .

Briggs let the man's body slump back on the control panel, then turned back to Graves. "The game has changed."

"What?"

"So far, everything that's happened here has been in accident. This one is murder. He's been shot."

"It's still Taranaga. I know it is!"

"Most likely. But now he's changing the rules."

"That doesn't make any sense, O'Meara. He has to know that we'll stop him if it becomes too obvious that the station is being sabotaged. I mean, up to now it's just been accidents. Nothing we could prove."

"Right," Briggs said. Taranaga had changed the rules in response to Briggs coming here. But what did he hope to gain by being so blatant?

Unless he wasn't being so blatant, the thought suddenly occurred to Briggs. He brushed past Graves and headed across the catwalk as fast as he could go.

"Hey!" Graves shouted behind him.

Briggs had just gotten to the elevator when a single shot sounded down in the jungle. "Shit!" he swore out loud. He was right. And he knew damned well what the shot had been.

Graves had ducked down, but Briggs waved him on. "That wasn't meant for us."

"What was it, then?" Graves asked.

The elevator came, and they both stepped on and took it down.

"Check your personnel roster. You're going to find that one of your people was becoming unstable. You'll find him out there with a bullet through his head."

"What?"

"It'll look like he took a high-powered rifle out into the jungle and took a pot shot at the base. He flipped out."

"Then the shot just now out in the jungle . . . he killed himself?"

"Right."

"Taranaga is off the hook again?"

"Right again."

"It'll read as a manifestation of the general superstition building here."

"Right again for the grand prize, Bob. He just sent us a message that he knew damned well who I am, and why I'm here."

"That, and the message that he's out to get you," Graves added as they reached the bottom.

84

Bower and Webb were waiting for them. "Did you hear the shot?" Webb asked.

"It's one of your people. He's killed himself."

"Killed himself . . ." Bower started, but then he looked up toward the control shack high above them. "How about Charlie?"

"Dead. Shot through the head. Your man went crazy."

Webb glanced at Briggs, and then he looked up at the control shack, and followed the line back out to the jungle. "Hell of a shot."

"Yup," Briggs said. He shook hands with them all. "Thanks for the instructive tour. I'm going back to town. I'm tired."

"Jesus H. Christ, you're not going back to town now! Not after what happened here!" Bower said.

"I have a feeling that with all your troubles out here, I'll be a hell of a lot safer in town," Briggs said. "Besides, I have to be around when Taranaga's invitation comes."

He rode back to his car with Graves. On the way down, the SIS man asked if Briggs wanted any backup.

"Absolutely not," Briggs said. "No matter what Taranaga *thinks,* he can't know yet that I'm not what I say I am."

"He can — and probably already has — checked with the magazine you supposedly represent in Canada."

Briggs smiled. "I hope he has, Bob. I hope he has. He'll be surprised."

At the car, out of earshot of the guards, Briggs

told Graves that he would be working alone. "From this point on, our only contact will come when it would be logical that you would talk to a Canadian journalist."

"Hardly ever."

"Right," Briggs said. He looked back up toward the camp. "Good luck here. I think you're going to need it. This may not happen overnight."

"We haven't been run off yet," Graves said. "But I'm beginning to think that Bower might have been right when he suggested you not accept an invitation from Taranaga."

"Come on, Graves. The only way we're ever going to find out for sure what's going on here is to push Taranaga, and push him hard. If he's innocent, nothing will happen. If he's behind this, I want to know why."

Graves looked at Briggs for several moments, then nodded. "Good luck," he said. "You're going to need it more than we are."

"Yeah," Briggs said.

The old Chevy started with some trouble, but then Briggs had it turned around on the dirt road and he headed back down to the island highway.

Off to the northeast, the jungle rose. Briggs glanced out that way. He wondered what, if anything, it was that Taranaga was hiding up there.

He came to the highway and accelerated toward town, a thick haze of blue smoke from the Chevy's exhaust curling around behind him.

He had just gotten here and already the opening salvos had been fired. In a way, he supposed, it was going to make his job easier. He wasn't going to have to goad Taranaga, or whoever had been behind the killing, into coming after him.

He also found that he was comparing this assignment to the ones he had been on in the Soviet Union, and to his life as a young man in Soho.

Then it had been Russians. They had been the ones who had murdered his mother. It was to them that he had directed his revenge. Here, on this island now, he found that he was not out for any kind of vendetta. Here, he was merely doing a job; one that he really wasn't interested in. Some old Japanese man who hated westerners was fighting for his own private little domain.

So what, Briggs found himself thinking.

He parked the Chevy in front of the hotel, then went inside where he dropped the keys on the front desk. The clerk was gone, and no one else seemed to be around.

Briggs's clothes clung to him in the heat. He went across the lobby into the tiny bar, where he rousted the barman from the back. He got half-dozen ice-cold bottles of Kirin — for his money, the only decent Japanese beer — and a large bucket with ice, and then took them upstairs.

He unlocked his door and pushed it open with his toe. He got halfway into the room, then stopped in his tracks.

A stunningly beautiful woman reclined on his bed, the pillows propped up behind her back, her long blond hair cascading down around her bare shoulders.

She wore a white, off-the-shoulder peasant dress, without stockings or jewelry. Her sandals lay on the floor beside the bed.

Her eyes were a lovely pale blue, and her complexion was creamy white. These were the tropics, but she had not been tanned. Rather than making her look sickly, however, her pale skin was sensuous.

"Hello," she said softly, her accent definitely American. Possibly Texan.

Briggs backed up and checked the number on his door. He stepped back in. "This is my room. Did room service send you up?"

She laughed. "No," she said. "I'm just a simple messenger girl."

Briggs came all the way in, closed the door behind him, and set the bucket of ice and beers on the table by the window. "A messenger girl. I'm beginning to like this island already."

She smiled at him, her teeth perfectly formed, pearly white, her lips very red by comparison although he could see that she wore little or no makeup.

"I've come to invite you to a cocktail party."

"I see," Briggs said. "Would you care for a beer. It's ice cold?"

"I'd love one," she said after a brief hesitation.

"Great," Briggs said. He got a couple of clean glasses from the bathroom and rinsed them out anyway, then opened a couple of beers. "You never did say your name."

"Gloria Conley," the girl said. "I'm a private secretary to Soshi Taranaga."

"I see," Briggs said, grinning. He brought her one of the beers. "Perhaps you can tell me why he's been causing so much trouble out at the British installation."

"Trouble?"

"Yes. The accidents. Like this afternoon. I could have been killed. Everyone knows it's Taranaga. But no one knows why. Can you enlighten me?"

"I don't know what you're talking about, Mr. Blake. Honestly."

Briggs had been looking into her eyes, paying very close attention. He believed her. "Do you travel with him, then?"

She shook her head. "No. I've been here, on this island, for several years now."

Briggs took a deep drink of the cold beer. He put the glass down, and lit himself a cigarette. She reached up and took it from him. He lit another.

"Forgive me, Gloria, if I'm a little dense. But you say you're a messenger from Taranaga. I'm being invited to a cocktail party tonight?"

"That's right."

"Then why didn't you just leave the message downstairs? What are you doing up here in my room, like this."

She laughed, her voice light, almost musical. "Taranaga-san wanted to make sure that you were coming. He told me to see to it. I was told by my friends that you were a man of immensely good looks. A Canadian. I wanted to see for myself."

"And?"

"My friends were right," she said smiling. "Will you join us for cocktails—and dinner of course—this evening? Black tie?"

Briggs had to smile. Whoever, or whatever, she really was, her smile was infectious, and she was a gorgeous creature.

"I wouldn't miss it for the world," Briggs said. "Now, if you will excuse me, I must take a shower. It's been a beastly day."

"Go right ahead, Mr. Blake, don't let me intimidate you," Gloria said. She looked as if she were genuinely enjoying herself.

"All right," Briggs said. He peeled off his khaki shirt, and Gloria sucked her breath when she saw the half-dozen scars on his torso, two of them obviously bullet wounds. For some reason women found his scars fascinating.

He went into the bathroom, got the shower going, then peeled off the rest of his clothes and stepped under the blissfully cool spray.

A couple of minutes later, the curtain parted, and Gloria, nude now, the slight tuft of hair at her pubis just as blond as the hair on her head, stepped in with him.

"Is this part of the personal invitation service?" Briggs asked.

"No," she said, turning him around and starting to wash his back. "I'm off duty now. These are my own hours."

"I see," Briggs said. "I'm really starting to like this island a lot."

They made love on the large bed directly after their shower, without bothering to dry off. A slight breeze had sprung up and came through the window, cooling them.

From the moment they'd begun, Gloria had taken

charge. It was obvious to Briggs that she had been more than Taranaga's private secretary here on the island. Much more.

Part of the old man's file had indicated that he had one weakness — besides his dislike for westerners — and that was for unusual and exotic sexual literature, devices, and practices.

He had apparently taught Gloria well, because she worked tirelessly on Briggs, doing things to his entire body, to every orifice, that he did not think were possible, and that he had never thought could give any pleasure.

After an hour — not of lovemaking but of mechanizations, he thought — Gloria got up and looked down at him, a slight smile on her lips, her body shining with perspiration.

"It was nice, Mr. Blake?"

Briggs grinned and nodded. "I doubt if I'll be able to move for a week or so, but sure, it was nice."

"That makes me happy," she said insincerely.

Briggs propped himself up on one elbow and waited until she came back from a very quick shower.

"They didn't teach you that sort of thing in Texas," he said while she was getting dressed.

She laughed, the sound again light. "Oh no, not that in El Paso." She laughed again.

"You know that I'm here to deal with your boss," Briggs said on impulse, when she was finished and at the door ready to leave

She turned back and looked at him. "I know," she said. "Everyone on the island knows. It is — as they say — delicious."

"Is that why you came here like this?"

"Oh yes, of course," she said, and then she was gone, leaving Briggs to wonder exactly which way she had meant her answer.

He got up, and the door opened without a knock. Gloria stuck her head inside. "A car will come to fetch you at six-thirty sharp. You will be ready?"

"Sure will."

"You have a tuxedo?"

"Never travel without one."

She smiled, and left again.

Briggs stared at the door for a long time, thinking about her, about what she had done here, and he finally had to shake his head. There was no way in which Gloria could be compared with Sylvia Hume. Gloria Conley was a machine programmed for sex: a gorgeous, smiling, efficient machine, but Briggs suspected an unhappy one. On the other hand, Sylvia could always be summed up in one word: She was a *lady*.

He opened a cold beer, drained half of it, then went into the bathroom and took another shower, this one as cold as it would get, and lasting a long time, a very long time indeed, as if he were very dirty.

He was dressed and ready by six o'clock. It had been suggested before the trip that he take along evening clothes on the chance that what was happening tonight would indeed happen, that he would be invited to Taranaga's for drinks and dinner.

"You'll need to dress for it. Taranaga will probably be in his formal Japanese traditional costume, and it will be expected that you be appropriately dressed," he had been told.

He had fixed his stiletto in its sheath at the small of his back. He buttoned his tuxedo jacket and looked at himself in the mirror. A little too craggy, he thought, but still not so bad.

Downstairs, he entered the bar and ordered himself an Irish whiskey. The Polynesian bartender gave him rye, but Briggs drank it anyway, lighting a cigarette and looking around the dim room.

There were a few others here already, including the pilot and copilot of the transport he had come in on from Port Moresby.

He waved to the copilot, who had walked from the plane into the customs shed with him, but the man turned away as if he had not seen the gesture.

The copilot was most likely in Taranaga's employ. It was why he had been interested in Briggs at the airport. Not because the man was with the SIS.

Briggs had to smile at his own näiveté, as he turned back to his drink. He finished it and ordered another one.

The desk clerk came to the doorway, spotted Briggs, and came over.

"Mr. Blake, there is a telephone call for you, sir," the clerk said. He was the same man Briggs had jinxed earlier. He was very respectful now, and he held his distance.

"Can I take it in here?"

"Yes, sir, of course," the clerk said. He said something in polygot Polynesian to the barman, then turned and went back out into the lobby, probably to the switchboard to transfer the call.

The barman brought Briggs's second drink with

the telephone. It rang and Briggs picked it up.

"Yes," he said. "S. Rupert Blake here."

"Mr. Blake, this is Mr. Bower, the British receiving station manager. We met this afternoon."

"Oh yes, of course, Mr. Bower. To what do I owe the pleasure of your call? Did you wish the Sunday service after all?"

"Yes, that too," Bower said, flustered. "But the real reason I'm calling is that I understand you have been invited to Mr. Taranaga's home for cocktails and dinner this evening."

"Yes, I have," Briggs said. Careful now, he thought.

"Well, good. So have I. I was just calling to ask if you wanted me to come into town to pick you up. We could drive out together."

"Thank you, Mr. Bower, but no. My transportation should be here momentarily."

"I see," Bower said, again flustered. "Well . . . I shall see you out there a little later then."

"Yes," Briggs said, and Bower hung up.

Seven

A very small Japanese man in traditional costume showed up with a Cadillac limousine in front of the hotel precisely at six-thirty. The desk clerk came in to fetch Briggs, who paid the bartender and sauntered outside, where the driver bowed low, holding the rear door open.

Briggs slid inside, and moments later they were moving sedately out of town on the island's single highway.

It was a lovely evening, so Briggs asked the driver to shut off the air-conditioning, and he powered his window down.

He was still tired from traveling, from the close call out at the base, and from the strenuous love-making this afternoon. At this moment he wanted nothing more than to have a simple dinner, then crawl into bed, alone, and sleep for a few days. But tonight was too golden an opportunity for him to pass up.

He sat back after lighting himself a cigarette and relaxed, enjoying the breeze. On the back side of the front seats there was a wood-faced cabinet. A liquor locker, Briggs supposed. He reached out and opened it, exposing a row of three bottles: One was the same rye he had been served at the hotel, the second was a very good Irish whiskey, and the third was a very good Russian vodka.

It was just a little disconcerting to realize that Taranaga knew so much about him, and was toying with him like this.

The man was obviously power mad. It would, Briggs supposed, be an eventual key to his downfall. But meanwhile, he was still left with the puzzle as to why Taranaga was risking so much just to bother a British satellite receiving station. It simply made no sense.

They passed the turnoff for the satellite station and continued along the paved road, which rose up toward the foothills of the volcano, eventually passing the spot where Briggs had stopped earlier.

The road curved around over a final hill, and the land flattened out onto a broad, well laid-out compound surrounding a central clearing, in the middle of which was a large, lovely rock garden and fountain.

The buildings all were built among the trees, but all were subordinate to a very large, rambling house set back from the square or plaza. There were several cars and jeeps parked in front of the house. Briggs figured that every vehicle that wasn't an earthmover on the island had to be parked there. A helicopter was parked off to one side.

Paper lanterns were hung everywhere through the trees. Strolling Japanese musicians moved throughout the property. And many well-dressed people strolled here and there, past tables ladened with food and the scattered bars with attendant barmen.

The Cadillac limo pulled up in front of the broad veranda at the front of the house, and a footman came down and opened the rear door for Briggs.

He was directed up the wide stairs and across the broad veranda into the house, where two members of the house staff were waiting. They bowed deeply, and Briggs returned in kind.

They led him back through the house to where Gloria Conley, dressed in a stunning evening gown, a diamond tiara in her hair, with just a hint of makeup, a lovely diamond bracelet on her right wrist, was waiting.

"Good evening, Mr. Blake, welcome to our home," she said pleasantly, her white teeth flashing.

"Good evening, Miss Conley, you're looking lovely tonight."

"Thank you," Gloria said. She stepped aside, took Briggs by his arm, and led him the rest of the way through the house, and out a sliding door to a very stark, long narrow room. The only things in the room were a lantern hanging from the low ceiling, a single painting on one translucent wall, and a dozen pairs of thonged slippers in a line. "Beyond this point you may not wear street shoes, Mr. Blake. I hope you will understand."

"Of course," Briggs said. He slipped off his formal pumps, and stepped into a pair of slippers. Gloria did the same.

"Taranaga-san would like very much to meet and speak with you before he appears at his party," Gloria said when they were ready. "I hope you do not mind."

"On the contrary. I'm flattered that he wishes to speak on such intimate terms with a Canadian journalist sent to do a story on him."

She smiled. "This way," she said, sliding open a broad rice-paper door.

They stepped out onto a wide veranda that was shaped like a large U, with a lovely rock garden, fountains, and goldfish ponds in its center.

Soshi Taranaga was seated, cross-legged, at a very low table at the far end of the dimly lit veranda. He was alone.

They approached him, and Gloria stopped a few respectful feet away.

Taranaga was a very old man, his skin hung in folds around his neck. His hands were gnarled, and blue veins crisscrossed his face.

He seemed to be in a trance. A tiny bowl of incense, on a small, lacquered table beside him, sent curls of smoke upward, perfuming the night air.

A third table beside Taranaga contained an alcohol warmer, a saki serving bottle, and two saki cups.

Taranaga's eyes fluttered; he blinked, swallowed several times, then turned and looked up at Briggs. He smiled, the gesture holding absolutely no warmth. He bowed his head slowly.

"Welcome to my humble home, Mr. . . ." he hesitated a moment. "S. Rupert Blake?"

"Yes, that's right," Briggs said, barging forward

and sticking out his hand.

Taranaga just looked up at him, his eyes narrowing. Gloria gasped. Briggs laughed inwardly.

"Er . . . well, pardon me. I didn't know . . ."

"Please, Mr. Blake, have a seat," Taranaga said.

Briggs sank down across the low table from Taranaga, and Gloria immediately got on her knees, pouring saki in both cups and bringing them over.

Taranaga raised his saki cup in salute, Briggs followed suit, and they both drank. The rice liquor was warm, but not hot. It was delicious. Gloria poured them each another.

"Why are you on Swanson Island?" Taranaga asked.

Briggs sipped at his second saki. He grinned at the Japanese man. "A direct question, for a man such as yourself."

"I have found that directness is often a virtue like a double-edged sword."

"A peculiarly western notion, don't you agree?" Briggs said.

Taranaga's nostrils flared, but he had wonderful self-control. This was quite different from the blunt behavior of the Russians, Briggs thought.

"When one deals with westerners, one must adopt certain of their oddities."

"In one's own home? How strange," Briggs said, still baiting the man. He finished his saki. Gloria scooted over and filled his cup. Taranaga drained his, and she filled it.

"I will ask you again, Mr. Blake, why have you come to Swanson Island?"

"By now, no doubt, you know exactly who I am,

and why I am here. It is no secret. I have come to investigate your life."

"Do you feel no danger in such an undertaking?"

"Heavens, no, should I?" Briggs said, wide-eyed.

Taranaga stared at him for a long time. Then he finished his saki. Briggs drank his, and Taranaga got to his feet. Briggs got up, too.

"It is time for us to join the others, Mr. Blake. I am happy we had this little talk."

"So am I. I would like to make another appointment with you for—"

"After this evening, Mr. Blake, we shall not be meeting each other again."

"I'm sorry, sir, I really wanted to talk to you—"

"That will not be possible," Taranaga interrupted.

"—about the war," Briggs finished it.

Taranaga's eyes got round. Blood came to his face. For a moment, Briggs thought the old man was going to have a stroke. But he was a study in self-control. He squared his shoulders.

"That was a very long time ago, Mr. Blake. I hope you do not still hold grudges against me and my countrymen."

Briggs smiled. Gotcha, you bastard, he thought. "I was actually thinking less of the war, and more of the periods just before and directly afterward."

"Whatever for?"

"You were a traditionalist before the war, a fierce competitor in the western world of finance afterward, and now you seem to be returning to your traditional values. Godless values, I might add. As a westerner affected by the electronic marvels your companies are building, I would like to understand you better. My readers, good Christians all, would like to understand as well."

"You will have to speculate, Mr. Blake, for I will not grant you an interview."

Briggs started to protest, but Taranaga held up his hand.

"Now, I suggest we join my guests for cocktails. Perhaps we could think of this tonight as . . . your farewell party."

Briggs bowed. Taranaga, almost reflexively, returned the gesture, then turned and stalked imperiously off toward the front of the house, leaving Briggs and Gloria alone on the veranda.

She got to her feet. She was shaking. "You should not have done that."

"Done what, sweetheart?" Briggs asked. He stepped away from the table, and went to one of the sliding doors. He opened it.

"Here . . . you can't do that," Gloria protested.

Briggs ignored her, stepping inside a small, well-furnished room. Low tables were laden with books and papers, while the walls held lovely Japanese paintings. One table contained a collection of brushes, an ink pot, and a stack of fine writing paper.

This was evidently Taranaga's study. Possibly even his inner sanctum. Briggs wished he could read Japanese.

"He will kill you, if he finds that you have been here. Believe me when I say that."

Briggs glanced at her. "He's already tried, Gloria."

She shook her head in irritation. She didn't believe him.

Briggs crossed the room, and carefully slid open the far door. In the distance, he could faintly hear the sounds of music and laughter and talking. He would not be able to snoop around very long before Taranaga would send someone to look for him.

He opened the door the rest of the way and stepped out into a narrow corridor. Left was toward the main part of the house; right was farther back. Briggs turned right, and opened the door for the next chamber across the corridor.

Gloria was directly behind him and she tried to pull him back, but it was too late.

Briggs stood on the threshold of Taranaga's playroom. There were mirrors on the ceiling and bondage chains hanging from the walls. A large, low bed set on a broad dais occupied the center of the room. The sheets were mussed and stained with blood. Taranaga was fastidious about everything in his home, except this room. The blood was a mark of honor for him.

There were whips, and daggers, and other instruments of torture.

Briggs turned slowly to face Gloria, who had shrunk back out into the corridor.

"He takes you . . . into this room? Is this where . . . you do it?"

Gloria's eyes began to glisten. "You don't understand," she said.

"I think I do," Briggs said. He turned and continued down the corridor, looking in room after room. One was a ceremonial tea room, another a simple linen closet, and still another Taranaga's personal sleeping quarters.

Finally, the corridor ended with a door that led

outside, across a narrow compound serviced by a road that was blocked off by a gate, to a low, rambling building without windows, and with only one broad door.

"What is that place?" Briggs asked Gloria.

"I don't know," she said. "He never allows anyone from inside the house out here. Never."

"Wait here," Briggs said.

"Mr. Blake," Gloria protested, but he ignored her. He crossed the compound and ducked around the side of the building, out of her sight for just a moment, until he had slipped his stiletto out of its sheath at the small of his back. Then he stepped back, and blocking what he was doing with his body, quickly picked the big padlock on the door.

"Mr. Blake?" Gloria called again. She remained within the corridor. "Please," she cried. "We must go back to the others."

"Just a moment," Briggs said. He opened the door and groped inside, finally finding a light switch to the right, and he flipped it on, flooding the expansive room with light.

Briggs let out a low whistle. Any last lingering doubts he may have had about Taranaga's complicity in the harassment of the British satellite receiving base left him. The building was filled with armaments. Tons of the stuff; it had to be worth millions of dollars—everything from Israeli Uzi machine guns to Soviet-built Kalashnikov assault rifles to American M16 automatic rifles. Hand grenades, 50-caliber and bigger machine guns, mortars, and gas masks lined the walls, filled shelves, and were packed in crates stacked in the middle of the floor. He figured there were enough arms and ammunition here in the building to fully equip a force of a few hundred men and allow them to fight for months.

Either Taranaga was totally off his rocker or he was planning a major siege on the base.

On the far side of the building, stacked against the wall that faced outward toward the slopes of the volcano, Briggs spotted a dozen crates of dynamite. Beside that was a shelf which held a mound of brick-shaped objects, each wrapped in heavy, brown waxed paper. It was *plastique*. Taranaga had thought of everything; if not a direct attack or a siege, then perhaps sabotage.

Briggs backed out of the armory after he had sheathed his stiletto, then closed and re-locked the door.

Gloria was greatly relieved when he rejoined her in the corridor. She did not ask him what he had found in the outer building. He supposed she either did not care, or was simply too frightened at the moment even to think about asking. It was a safe bet that Taranaga was using her for strange sexual practices. That was not at all unusual in the world. But he could not square that knowledge with what he knew of the young woman. She did not seem the type to go in for masochism.

They hurried down the corridor together, back through Taranaga's study, and then through to the front of the house where Taranaga was holding court in the midst of a dozen people, all of them well-dressed in traditional Japanese or Polynesian costume.

John Webb, the station's construction manager,

and Graves, the SIS man, both of them dressed in tuxedos, stood together across the veranda beside the service bar.

Briggs excused himself from Gloria, and went across to them.

"Good evening, gentlemen," Briggs said expansively.

Both men looked up and smiled. Webb was about to say something, but Graves cut him off.

"Ah, Mr. Blake, it's a pleasure to see you again so soon, sir."

They shook hands. Briggs got himself an Irish whiskey, straight up, no ice, no water, and then looked around at the other guests.

"Where is Mr. Bower? I thought he would be here this evening?"

"He's coming along," Graves said.

"Olsen and Veerhusen, two of our engineers, are coming with him. They had some last-minute items to go over before they left," Webb said. He glanced at his watch. "In fact, they should be here any minute now."

"Bower telephoned me earlier, and asked if he could come into town to give me a lift."

"Taranaga sent a car for you?" Graves asked.

Briggs nodded. They glanced over at Taranaga, who looked up and caught Briggs's eye. He smiled.

"The bastard," Graves said under his breath.

Briggs turned back. "Careful now, you're a guest in his house."

"The son-of-a-bitching rotter is planning something. I know bloody well he is. And you can count on it not being very pleasant."

"Did you find your sharpshooter in the jungle?"

Graves blinked, but then nodded. "Yes," he said. "Rodney Harcourt. He put the rifle in his mouth and somehow managed to pull the trigger."

"Wasn't a particularly pretty sight," Webb said.

"What about his record? Anything in it about being a marksman? A member of a rifle team? Anything like that?"

Graves shook his head. "His friends say he hated guns. But he was into something."

"No one wants to talk about it."

"That's right. They're hiding something. But it doesn't have anything to do with Harcourt being some sort of an expert rifle shot."

"No," Briggs said. "If you want to dig into it you'll probably find that the poor sod got involved somehow in smuggling. It brought him into town quite a bit, where Taranaga's people could work on him, screw him up in the head. They lured him out into the woods and killed him. Simple."

"You're right of course—" Graves had started to say, when one of the base jeeps came screeching to a halt just below the veranda.

"It's Tim Ahern," Webb said.

The young-looking man leaped out of the jeep, and raced up onto the porch, spotting Webb, Graves, and Briggs immediately. Everyone else at the party stopped talking and turned to see what the commotion was all about.

"Oh, Christ, Mr. Webb, Mr. Graves; you have to come quickly."

Graves put his drink down. "What is it, Tim? What's happened?"

"It's Mr. Bower and the others," Ahern said breathlessly.

"What about them?" Graves asked. "They're supposed to be here by now. Where are they? Has there been some trouble out at the base?"

"No, sir. On the road coming up here," Ahern said.

"What is it?" Graves shouted.

Briggs knew what was coming. He glanced over to where Taranaga had been standing, but the Japanese man was gone. He was nowhere to be seen on the veranda.

"It was an accident. Their jeep skidded off the road, turned over in the ditch, and burned. It was horrible."

"They're dead?" Webb asked incredulously.

"Yes, sir. They burned to death. My God—it was . . . horrible."

Eight

Webb jumped into the front of the jeep with Ahern, the young engineer, while Briggs and Graves got in the back. They raced away from Taranaga's home and out of the compound.

As soon as they were out of sight of the house, Briggs tapped Ahern on the shoulder and motioned for him to pull over.

"What is it?" Graves shouted.

Briggs ignored him. "What about Bower and the others?" he asked the young engineer. "Are you certain they're dead?"

"Yes, sir," Ahern said, nodding. It looked as if he was on the verge of being sick. The accident must have been gruesome.

"What happened? Exactly."

Ahern looked from Graves to Webb and back again. "I was following them, when their jeep . . . just started swerving all over the place. It crashed into the ditch and just exploded." The young man shook his head. "It was horrible."

"You won't find anything until the fire cools down," Briggs told Graves. "But when it does, and you can get a good look at the jeep, you'll probably find that the steering mechanism was tampered with. That, and somehow the fuel line was set to come apart on impact, spraying fuel all over the hot manifold."

"Let's go, then," Webb said, turning around.

Briggs got out of the jeep.

"Where the hell—" Webb started.

"Check out the jeep, then get your doctor out to take care of the bodies. When you're finished, get back to the base and stay there," Briggs said. He glanced back up the road toward Taranaga's compound. "I think something big is going to happen tonight." He turned back. "So be ready for anything."

Graves nodded. "What about you?"

"I have a little more snooping around to do. I'll be out to the base later."

"I don't think you should go back up there," Graves said. "I think we should just call in the Royal Marines."

"To do what?" Briggs shouted. "Taranaga will have an ironclad alibi for every single thing that's happened and will happen on this island."

"He can't get away with this, sir," Ahern interjected.

Briggs grinned. "You're damned right he can't get away with it. You're damned right." He hit the side of the jeep. "Now get the hell out of here."

Ahern turned back to the wheel, but before the jeep had gone ten yards, Briggs had disappeared into the dense jungle.

Taranaga would not be expecting him to return so soon, and not like this; his guard would be at its lowest just at this moment.

No doubt the party was still going on, and would continue until late.

Of course he would have sentries posted as a routine. Briggs had not seen them within the compound, but he was almost certain that the perimeter would be guarded.

The thick undergrowth at the side of the road thinned out farther in, and within a hundred yards, the going was relatively easy.

Briggs pulled off his tie, unbuttoned his top shirt button, and discarded his jacket. He pulled out his stiletto, the razor-sharp blade gleaming in a stray bit of starlight.

Taranaga was behind all the killings and destruction. There was not enough evidence to convict the man in an international court of law, but there was plenty to convince Briggs, who had seen it written plainly in the man's eyes.

Sweat was pouring off him by the time he came within sight of the compound lights. Holding his breath, he could hear the sounds of laughter and talking and bits of music drifting down to him on the breeze. The party was going full swing as if nothing untoward had happened.

Cautious now, since he was this close, Briggs moved slowly up the hill, his every sense alert for any sign of the posted sentries that he was sure were there.

Taranaga excused himself from the small knot of Japanese businessmen he had been speaking with, and went into the house.

Nakasuri Ogi was just coming from the rear of the house. He had a deeply concerned look on his face.

"Where is Miss Conley?" Taranaga demanded. He had been looking for her ever since the British had left to scrape their station manager and his two foolish engineers out of the burnt remains of the jeep.

"I do not know, Taranaga-san. I presumed she was on the veranda with you."

"She was. But she is gone now. I want her found!"

"Of course, Taranaga-san. But there is something of importance that you must know."

Taranaga had looked beyond Ogi, but something in the man's voice and manner made him understand that something important was happening. He turned back.

"What is it?" he snapped impatiently.

"It is the man who calls himself Blake. The Canadian journalist."

"What about him?"

"He's just come through the A-marker."

Taranaga grinned. "Are you sure, Ogi? Are you absolutely certain it was him?"

"Yes, Taranaga-san. He tripped the perimeter alarm, so the infrared cameras automatically turned on him. I saw him. It is Blake."

"On his way here. To see me." Taranaga grinned even harder. "Then we shall provide a reception for him the moment he breaks through to the compound."

Taranaga and Ogi hurried to the rear of the house, and behind Taranaga's private quarters, they slid apart a section of wall that held a watercolor of Mount Fuji. Inside was a large room filled with complicated electronic equipment, most of it monitoring and communications gear for the compound.

One set of screens, that should have been showing a section of the compound's perimeter to the southwest, was blank.

Ogi punched several buttons, which caused green lights to wink on. But then he looked up, puzzled. "The equipment is working. But there is no picture."

Taranaga shoved the man aside, and his fingers flew over the controls to the cameras guarding the perimeter. There was nothing on the screens, however, even though the equipment seemed to be working properly.

"You are sure it was the one called Blake?" Taranaga asked.

"Positively, sir. I saw him with my own eyes."

Taranaga stared thoughtfully at the blank screens. "Then he has somehow sabotaged our cameras. Interesting."

"Shall I call out our defenses?"

Taranaga thought a moment. "I think not. At least not just yet. So far, Blake can only suspect me. Let him find more. Let's see just why he has come back." He reached out and flipped a series of switches. The screens lit up now, showing various views of the interior of the compound and the area immediately surrounding the house. One screen showed an overhead view of the armory in the back.

Taranaga went across the room, and from a drawer extracted a tiny radio receiver with an earphone that looked just like a hearing aid.

He put it on, and then flipped a switch on the console in front of the screens.

"Keep watch here. I am returning to my party. When Mr. Blake shows up, I will want to know where he is and exactly what he is doing."

"Yes, Taranaga-san."

"In addition, I wish you to send out two runners: one immediately to the British receiving station to inform my ninja to hurry their task and return here without delay."

"And the second, sir?"

"The second runner I want to search for Miss Conley. Wherever she is, I want her returned to me."

"Yes, Taranaga-san."

Taranaga left the surveillance-communications center, and returned to the veranda at the front of his house, the sounds of music and laughter light on this ears. Soon, very soon, he told himself, the island would once again be all his, and his secret would be safe.

There almost certainly were other cameras placed throughout the compound. Evidently, they were not manned at all times, otherwise Taranaga would have known that Briggs had seen the armory, and he would certainly have done something about it.

It meant, simply, that the system, though very sophisticated, was fallable. He just wondered if anyone had been watching the cameras he had spotted in the trees before he had covered the lenses with dirt.

He had come up from the southwest. He angled almost due north now, nearly parallel to the inner perimeter fence that blocked off the entire northeastern end of the island.

It had to be four miles to the north beach, at least, but Briggs had no intention of going that far.

Through the jungle to his right, he could hear the sounds of talk and music, and see the vague outlines of the buildings within the compound, including Taranaga's house itself.

The armory was at the rear of the main house, to its northeast, just below the slopes that led up to the volcano, now dark, that hung over this end of the island like some sort of brooding giant.

The tall, wire-mesh fence was a few yards to his right. He was sure it was electrified, although there were no signs posted to that effect. But the jungle had been cut away a few yards on either side of the fence to stop branches waving in the wind from hitting the wire and shorting out the current to ground.

The sounds of the party died gradually away, and soon Briggs could no longer catch even a glimpse of a light through the jungle.

He figured he had come well north of the house, and probably the entire compound. From what he had seen earlier, Taranaga's house was the furthermost building from the road. There could have been others, deeper into the jungle, but Briggs had not caught sight of them, nor could he detect any lights shining from that direction now.

He began looking for a tall tree with overhanging branches fairly close to the fence. He found one almost immediately, although all of its branches facing the fence had been cut severely back.

From the ground, the distance did not look too far. He climbed the tree until he reached a point a few feet above the top of the fence. From there, it looked like a couple of miles to the other side.

Back toward the south he could see lights, but he could hear nothing of the party. Instead, he could just hear the very faint sounds of the surf on the rock cliffs and beach, and the wind blowing through the tops of the trees. It was a very lonely sound. One that he was not used to. He had always been a city person. He had been born and raised in London, a city much like New York in that it never slept. There were always trucks and cars and the occasional sirens somewhere far off in the distance. Wind and surf were sounds of no civilization. Lonely.

He crawled out on the stump of a branch, the entire tree bending under his weight.

There were probably a couple of thousand volts running through the fence. Enough to easily fry a man. The jolt would come so instantaneously on contact that he wouldn't feel a thing.

"Piss on it," he muttered, and he leaped out, head first, in a tightly tucked dive. He was conscious of passing very closely over the fence, and then he was falling, twisting his body around in an effort to land feet first, his right hand holding the stiletto out away from his body.

He hit on his left shoulder, his entire arm going instantly numb, and then he was rolling, crashing into the underbrush, coming finally to a halt.

For a long time Briggs lay there, spread-eagled, listening to the absolute lack of jungle sounds. The night-hunting birds had been screeching before; the insects had been singing their song. All was still now, except for the crashing surf in the distance.

If Taranaga had placed any ultrasensitive sound pickups out here, he knew that something big had crashed through the underbrush.

Briggs got up, mentally exploring his body. Nothing was broken, although by morning his shoulder and the ribs on his left side would be damned sore.

Back at the narrow clearing beside the fence, Briggs got his bearings and then struck out in a diagonal line through the jungle, toward where he figured the back of Taranaga's house should be located.

Even from deep within the jungle, he could look up and from time to time catch a glimpse of the tall volcano above.

Within ten minutes, Briggs was again hearing the sounds of the party. And five minutes later he came to the edge of the compound's clearing. He had made his angle just a little wide, and had come out a hundred yards above the back of the house.

He could see across the entire compound, but he could not see the front veranda of Taranaga's house, although that was where all the music, most of the light, and most of the talking and laughter were coming from.

Ducking back into the protection of the jungle, Briggs carefully worked his way back to a spot just behind the armory.

He got down on his stomach and crawled the last few yards to the edge of the clearing, and then lay there, watching.

The armory was protected by a tall wooden fence. Since it was within the compound, Briggs figured the fence was more a warning for the staff to stay out than an actual security barrier.

Beyond the armory shed, the main house rose. On a tall tripod, silhouetted above the roofline, was a camera. It looked down on the armory. Someone could be watching this place.

Briggs worked his way farther back, away from the armory, but closer in to the house itself. There was no one here. He listened, but could hear nothing other than the now-faint sounds of the party at the front.

He got up and quickly crossed the narrow clearing to the house, where he leaped up, catching the eaves, and hauled himself up onto the low, gently sloped roof.

The house was very lightly built, and as Briggs worked his way to the backside of the camera mount, the roof beams sagged under his weight. He was half-afraid that he would crash through the roof.

At the camera, he pulled out his stiletto and quickly cut the transmission and power cable. A tiny spark sputtered at the end of the severed wires, then died.

There would be a power failure alarm to each camera, Briggs supposed. Which meant that someone would be coming back here to investigate very soon.

He hung over the edge of the roof, and dropped down into the area between the rear door of the house and the armory shed.

Without hesitation he hurried across to the shed, and using his stiletto quickly picked the padlock.

Inside, he grabbed one of the Israeli Uzi submachine guns and a couple of clips of ammunition, then stepped back out of the shed, re-locked the door, and hurried around to the tall wooden fence.

He slung the Uzi over his shoulder, stuffed the two extra banana clips of ammo into his belt, and scrambled over the fence to the other side, disappearing into the woods as the rear door of the house opened.

He dove into the jungle, rolled left, and then lay still.

The sounds of the party still came from the front, but there was nothing else to hear. Gradually, Briggs sat up, made sure the Uzi was on automatic and ready to fire, then crossed back through the clearing to the rear of the building.

Someone would be coming to see what had happened to the camera. He wanted to wait until they had come and gone before he continued. He wanted to see if the compound's security system was actually being monitored.

He stopped at the back of the armory shed and listened, but he could hear nothing, so he eased along the building until he came to the fence.

He slung the Uzi over his shoulder, and was about to jump up on the fence when something very large and very heavy landed on him from above, sending him sprawling. But before he had a chance to do much of anything, something hit him in the side of the head and neck.

He managed to shove his attacker off and roll to the right, but as he did, something that felt like a twenty-ton lead weight slammed into his testicles. The excruciating pain bounced off the inside of his skull, echoing within his head as if he were the Grand Canyon.

Briggs swung out blindly, his right hook connecting with something soft. A split instant later two hammer blows smashed into his side, cracking at least one of his ribs with an audible pop.

"Christ," Briggs swore, falling backward.

He finally saw his assailant. He was an exceedingly well-built Japanese man, barefoot and wearing black pajamas—who was coming at him again. Briggs kicked out with his shoe, catching the man just below the right eye.

Instead of falling back, and getting the hell out of there, Briggs sprung forward, swinging his right hook with all his might, connecting with Ogi's chin, snapping the man's head backward.

Briggs jumped up and started to bring the gun around, but the tenacious Japanese had leaped to his feet and charged, three vicious karate blows landing on Briggs's shoulder and right side.

Again, Briggs slammed a right hook into the man's face, then a left, another right, and finally a powerhouse of a left, and Ogi went down.

This time he stayed down.

Briggs was on the verge of collapse. His entire body felt like it was on fire, as if it had been pulverized.

He stumbled backward, falling into the underbrush. It took him a minute or so to untangle himself and get back to his feet. He turned and started to stumble away, but then he looked back.

The Japanese man still lay on his back, out cold. Briggs could not leave him there. Not like that.

He went back, and pulling the man by his right arm, dragged him yard by yard back into the jungle, until they were about fifty yards away from the armory. Ogi began to come around. He had started to sit up when Briggs hit him with every ounce of his strength, a perfect right hook to the chin. Ogi went down.

Briggs stumbled back closer to the clearing, to a spot where he could see the rear wall of the armory.

The dynamite and *plastiques* were stacked against the rear wall.

Briggs raised the Uzi submachine gun to his shoulder, clicked the safety off, and, aiming for the center of the armory's rear wall, fired a short burst.

His hits stitched across the back wall, and an instant later the entire night was lit by a tremendous fireball, the concussion rolling back up the hill, flattening the jungle and sending Briggs flying fifteen yards into the undergrowth.

Nine

Flames leapt high into the night sky, and an occasional round still popped off, but by the time Briggs regained consciousness, most of the fireworks were over.

He lay in the underbrush, the sounds of the fire and of people shouting coming to him.

They were fighting the fierce fire. He could see that, his eyes slowly coming back into focus. His body felt like it had been used as a battering ram.

He rolled over, crawled to the edge of the thicket of brush, and looked down at the fire. A large section of the back of Taranaga's house had been destroyed in the initial blast, and another section was on fire.

Guests from the party were pouring water on the blaze from a half-dozen hoses, and by the looks of it, they would have the fire out very soon.

Whatever plans Taranaga had had for the arms

and ammunition would have to be changed now, because it was all gone.

Given time, of course, the armory would be replaced. But Briggs was not going to give the man time. Whatever was going to happen, Briggs resolved, was going to happen tonight.

Briggs crawled out of the underbrush, his side aching where his rib had been cracked, and worked his way around to the far side of the house, well away from the fire.

There was no one on the front veranda. Even the musicians had gone around to the back of the house, either to watch, or to help fight the blaze.

Briggs angled across the clearing, around the central rock garden and fountain, to where the cars were parked in a ragged row. The keys were in all of them.

He took one of the jeeps, started the engine, and then spun around and peeled out of the compound, down the road, and careened down the highway toward the receiving station.

Taranaga would not take this lying down, of course. He would have to retaliate against the base. The time had passed for them to investigate the man. It was time now for the Royal Marines as Graves had suggested.

Hope-Turner would know what to do, what strings to pull, to have reinforcements airlifted in within hours.

Briggs did not think they would have much longer than that. Although it was still a puzzle to him how Taranaga planned to cover up his attack, there was no doubt that it would come this night.

Either Taranaga was going to win this night, or Briggs was. There'd be no stalemate.

A shadowy figure raced across the highway a hundred yards ahead, and disappeared into the brush. Briggs's first thought was that it had been a deer, or some other large jungle animal.

A second later a half-dozen other dark figures crossed the road, just beyond the beams of the jeep's headlights. This time, however, Briggs knew damned well that they were not deer or any large jungle animal; they were men—Taranaga's men. And in the direction they had been going, back toward Taranaga's compound, they could only have been coming from one place: the satellite receiving station.

Briggs sped up, passing the spot where the men had crossed, and a couple of miles later he came to the turnoff to the station.

Flames were shooting up into the air from a large fire on the base. He could see it from here.

"Christ," he swore, pounding the steering wheel with the palm of his hand as he raced up the dirt road. They had gotten Bower and the two engineers earlier in the evening, and now they had hit the base.

He only hoped that Graves, Webb and the young kid—Ahern—had been clear when the attack came.

The base's main gate was closed, and barricades had been placed twenty-five yards up from the road.

Briggs cautiously approached the wooden barriers, stopping the jeep and climbing out, his hands high over his head. He did not want to get shot by a nervous guard at this point.

Through the fence, up near the main receiving dishes, it looked as if one or two of the equipment buildings were on fire. Beyond that, near the edge of the cliff that overlooked the sea, the main communications tower and antenna was down in a crumpled heap.

That's what Taranaga's people had come here for tonight! To knock out base communications with the outside world.

Slowly, Briggs side-stepped through the barriers. It was fairly early in the evening yet, but he was very conscious of the passage of time.

Taranaga was certainly making his moves tonight. But he would have the advantage in the darkness. Which meant it was going to happen tonight . . . before dawn.

"That's far enough," someone shouted from up beyond the gate.

Briggs stopped in his tracks. "I'm Rupert Blake! Get Steve Graves down here, he knows me!"

"Are you armed?"

"I only have a knife!" Briggs shouted back. He had left the Uzi in the underbrush above Taranaga's armory. He hadn't been thinking. He realized now that he should have taken along. Someone here on the base could have used it, although there had only been a couple of spare clips for it.

"Come forward," the voice shouted from the darkness.

Briggs did as he was told, keeping his hands in plain sight well over his head.

He stopped a few feet from the gate. One of the guards came out. He held an American M16 at the ready.

"Mr. Blake?" he said.

"If you'll call Steve Graves down here, or John Webb . . . either of them will recognize me."

"I know you, sir," the guard said, relaxing. He slung the rifle over his shoulder, and unlocked the gate for Briggs.

Two other guards came from the shadows.

"What happened here?" Briggs asked, slipping into the base. The guards were very nervous. The one who had let him in kept eyeing the jungle on either side of the dirt road as he re-locked the gate.

"I don't know, for sure. We think it was townspeople came out and started raising hell here at the main gate, keeping us busy."

"There was a couple of big explosions up by the cliffs, and a second or two later the crowd was gone," one of the other guards said.

"Anyone hurt?" Briggs asked.

"Yes, sir. I think so," the one guard who had unlocked the gate said. "They took out the main receiver and the comm shed. Both of them . . . had on-duty personnel inside."

"They took out the comms tower too, sir," one of the other guards said. "Everything is out. No phone, no radio back home."

"Hang on, it'll be over by morning," Briggs said. "Did Steve Graves and the others get back here?"

"Yes, sir. But did you hear? Mr. Bower was killed in an accident."

"I heard," Briggs said. "Get on the phone and tell Graves I'm down here, to come fetch me. I don't want to wander around up there; someone might take a pot shot at me."

"Yes, sir," the guard said. He went back into his guardshack and telephoned.

Briggs stepped a few feet up the road so that he could get a better view of the destruction by the cliffs. The flames were beginning to die down. The figures he had seen crossing the road had done this. They were on their way back to Taranaga to report a successful mission. But Christ, how in hell did the man expect to get away with it? Even if he did overrun the base, even if his people totally wiped out everything here, the man had to know that more would come. The entire British Navy would be here if need be. Margaret Thatcher had proven that with the Falkland Islands business.

It deeply bothered Briggs. Taranaga was not an ignorant man. He knew all that. Which meant he had some other knowledge. Something up his sleeve. But what?

"Mr. Graves is on his way down, sir," the guard said, coming back out of the guardhouse.

"Thanks," Briggs said absently.

"Sir, I suggest you get out of sight now."

Briggs turned to the man. "It's all right now. Nothing is going to happen until later."

"Sir?"

"I suggest you fortify this gate and your position as much as possible. They'll be hitting us again tonight with everything they've got."

"I'm no bloody soldier," one of the others said.

A pair of headlights started down the road from the administration building. Briggs watched it come.

"Oh yes you are," he said to the young man. "At least for tonight you are."

Graves was alone. On the way back up to administration he shook his head. "They hit us hard, O'Meara," he said.

"What'd they take out?"

"All our communications with the outside world. We're stuck now, unless something can be jerry-rigged. But I doubt that'll happen."

"They get all the gear?"

Graves glanced at Briggs and nodded. "Seven of our technicians and engineers were on duty; they're all dead too, in addition to Joe Bower and the two engineers he was with."

They pulled up in front of the administration building, and Graves switched off the headlights and ignition. He turned to Briggs.

"What the hell happened up at Taranaga's after we left? What'd the sonofabitch do? How'd he act knowing we were getting hit?"

"I talked to him. He told me he wouldn't be speaking to me again. Said this would be my farewell party."

"The bastard."

Briggs reached out and patted the SIS man on the arm. "Listen to me, Steve. I got out of there and snuck around back. I found an armory. The bastard had been stockpiling arms and ammunition. He had enough to wipe this entire base off the map a dozen times over."

"I knew it!"

"Listen. I managed to destroy it. Everything is gone. All his weapons, his explosives. Everything. It went up in flames."

"They were hitting us, and you were nailing those bastards?" Graves asked.

Briggs nodded, and Graves smiled. "Sonofabitch," he said. "The bastard wants a fight, we'll give him one."

Graves hopped out of the jeep, and Briggs followed him around to Bower's office inside the administration building. John Webb was there, along with a half-dozen other men.

They all looked up when Graves and Briggs came in.

"I thought you'd be a goner for sure," Webb said, coming around the desk.

"He destroyed Taranaga's armory," Graves said triumphantly.

"The hell you say," Webb boomed. He and Briggs shook hands. Then he introduced the others, all of them engineers. "We're trying to figure out a way of setting up communications with London. We're going to need help."

"How about the telephone exchange in town?" Briggs asked.

"It's controlled by Taranaga. At this point, I doubt if we'd get within a hundred yards of the place. And even if we did, the moment a call started going through to London, or anywhere else for that matter, the bloody bastard would pull the plug."

"The airstrip?"

"Our plane's already gone. Nothing else there."

"A boat?"

"All controlled by Taranaga," Webb said.

"What the hell are you planning on doing then?"

"Like I said, Mr. Blake or whoever the hell you are, we're going to try to jerry-rig some kind of shortwave transceiver. And we're bloody well going to defend ourselves."

Briggs started to say something, but Webb held him off.

"Look, I don't mean to sound ungrateful, and all. If you actually did destroy Taranaga's armory—and I'm not saying you didn't—then thank you. But in the meantime, we've got work to do. If you want to help, we'd appreciate it."

"That's what I was sent for. But I don't think we should just wait here for the man to come to us."

"What do you mean?"

"I've destroyed his armory, burned a section of his house. It's time for us to go after him."

"We don't have the troops or the weapons," Graves said. "He's got us outnumbered."

"The best we can do is a holding action while we radio out for help," Webb said. "If that's not to your liking . . . well we understand. Just don't get in our way." He turned away, but then he turned back. "And tell your girlfriend that we won't let her back in. She's made her choice."

"My girlfriend?" Briggs asked, something clutching at his heart.

"Yeah, she was here earlier. Gloria Conley."

"She showed up here tonight?"

"That's right. Just before the attack," Webb said bitterly. "She said she had to talk to you. The gate guards told her you weren't here, that you were at Taranaga's."

"Where'd she go?"

"I don't know, and I don't care," Webb snapped.

"You stupid bastard. She's Taranaga's private secretary. If she was coming here, she was trying to warn us. Christ."

"Jesus," Webb swore, falling back. "I didn't know. I—"

"I've got to find her. She might have gone back into town," Briggs said. He turned to Graves. "Get this place set up to be defended. Watch the cliffs, they probably came in that way. But also round up as many volunteers as you can."

"For what?" Graves asked.

"When I get back we're going to hit Taranaga's compound, and hit it hard."

"You've got me," Graves said.

"And me," Webb chipped in.

"I'll see about the telephone exchange. I might be able to pull a fast one," Briggs said.

He left the office, Graves coming with him. They climbed into the jeep and Graves drove him back down to the main gate, the fire still burning in the rubble of the collapsed communication center.

"They might hit us again, before the main thrust," Briggs said, thinking out loud. "They'll try for the generators, to knock out our electrical power, and then our fuel supplies, probably the

131

dispensary, and maybe some of the vehicles."

"We'll keep watch."

At the main gate Briggs got out. The guards were there.

"If anything happens . . . if for some reason I can't get back here, convince Webb to hit Taranaga hard tonight. It's our only way out."

Graves looked at him in the dim light. "Take it easy," he said.

"Yeah," Briggs said.

He slipped out the gate, hurried up beyond the barriers, and climbed in his jeep. He got it started, turned it around on the road, and headed back out to the highway, not turning on the headlights.

Behind him, Graves watched until he was out of sight, then climbed back in his jeep and headed back up to administration.

The copra operation was deserted, but when Briggs approached the town, it seemed as if everything were normal, that nothing out of the ordinary had happened this night.

He drove through the town, slowly passing in front of the hotel. The front doors were open, and he caught a glimpse of the clerk behind to the counter. The bar just off the lobby was dimly lit, and Briggs was sure he had seen several people inside.

Everything seemed normal.

He turned around at the far end of the block and came back, parking just across from the hotel. He crossed the street and went inside.

The clerk spotted Briggs and started for the back room.

"Hold on there, mister," Briggs shouted, rushing across the lobby.

The clerk, his eyes wide, his nostrils flared, pulled up short. He turned and forced a huge, toothy grin. "Ah, Mr. Blake, what has happened? Has there been an accident?"

"Did a young woman come here looking for me?" Briggs asked.

The clerk shook his head, but Briggs knew damned well the man was lying. He could see it in his eyes.

Briggs pulled out his stiletto. "I asked you if a young woman came here tonight looking for me?"

The clerk's mouth moved, but no sounds came out. He glanced upward toward the rooms, and then, catching himself, looked back, his eyes even wider.

Briggs leaped over the counter, shoving the frightened clerk out of the way. In a tiny alcove behind the key slots was the hotel's small switchboard. Briggs located the main cable run, and sliced it neatly in two with his razor-sharp blade.

He came back around the counter. The clerk was cowering in the corner.

"If you are not right here, behind this counter, when I come back down, I will find you and slit your throat, and then put a terrible curse on your entire family. Do you understand?"

The clerk nodded. His Adam's apple bobbed up and down.

All of this had happened so quickly, and so quietly, that no one from the bar across the lobby knew that anything was going on.

Briggs jumped back over the counter, and took the stairs up two at a time. He stopped on the second-floor landing and peered down the corridor. The light was out. There were no sounds up here. None.

The storm shutter at the end of the corridor had been shut.

This was a setup. Briggs could almost feel it thick in the air. He shifted his stiletto between his hands, holding it lightly at last in his right.

He reached down and took off his shoes and stockings, then started down the corridor. Slowly. Carefully. Every sense alert for the slightest hint that the attack was coming.

The door to his room was a few inches ajar, but the angle was wrong for him to see anything inside.

He took a deep breath and let it out slowly, then kicked the door open and barged into the room, rolling left, then right, keeping low.

He slipped on something wet, went down on one knee and then held there, his blade at the ready, every muscle liquid, ready for battle.

For several long seconds there was nothing. No sound. No motion. Nothing.

Slowly he got to his feet and went back to the light switch. He flipped it on.

The room was a shambles. Someone had been here and there had been a fight. His right foot and right trouser leg were covered with blood from a very large puddle in the center of the room. He stared at it for a long time. Gloria had left Taranaga's when Briggs had disappeared. She had gone to the base looking for him; when she hadn't found him there, she had come here looking. In the meantime, Taranaga had sent someone after her.

"Taranaga," Briggs hissed, spinning around and racing back to the stairs.

Ten

Taranaga, his clothing torn and dirty, smudges of soot on his face, burns pockmarking his hands, strode into the large, low-ceilinged room. Eight of his ninja warriors had been waiting for him. They all bowed very low. Their respect immense.

The aging Japanese businessman looked at them with pure, venomous hate in his eyes—not for them, but for the one man on this island who had actually done him serious harm.

He screamed in Japanese: "Death to traitors!" Spittle flew from his lips.

"Death to traitors!" the ninja screamed.

A door opened, and Nakasuri Ogi, wearing a spotlessly white kimono, came slowly in with his head bowed and knelt down on the grass mat in front of Taranaga. His jaw was swollen and turning purple where Briggs had hit him.

"Behold the traitor," Taranaga screamed, "who

could not defend his master."

"Behold the traitor!" the ninja screamed.

Taranaga held out his burned hands, and one of the ninja handed him a ceremonial, long-handled samurai sword, its highly polished steel blade gleaming in the single overhead light.

Ogi was not going to be allowed to die like an honorable man at his own hand. He was going to die like a traitor.

Taranaga raised the blade very high.

"Traitor," the ninja chanted.

The blade flashed as Taranaga brought it down with every ounce of his strength, neatly severing his one-time trusted aide's head cleanly.

The head thumped to the mat, and rolled a few feet away while Ogi's body slumped forward, blood spurting everywhere, legs thumping, his bowels loosening.

"Traitor," the ninja chanted at the skull. Its eyes were still open. "Traitor," they chanted again.

"Death to the British bastards," Taranaga screamed.

"Death to the British," the ninja shouted.

Taranaga handed over the sword, and without a backward glance at his old friend's body, he left the room, crossed the narrow courtyard, and went through a gate that led directly into his private rock garden.

Inside, he leaned back against the wall of the tall, solid fence, and waited for his old heart to slow down. It had been beating so hard in his chest that he had thought it would surely burst.

His thoughts went to the grave up on the hillside.

His memories went back for a moment to before the war, when this island had truly been his. When the world had belonged to the Rising Sun.

But then the acrid smell of smoke intruded on his consciousness, and he could feel his anger rising again to the surface, threatening to make him lose all self-control at any moment.

He pushed away from the wall and strode across his garden, up onto the broad veranda, and into his bathhouse, which had been slightly damaged in the fire. His staff had temporarily repaired the room, so that it was clean and serviceable.

"Hai," he said loudly.

Without turning around, he knew that someone had come into the tiny room with him. And he knew her by her odor. He held his arms out.

Gloria Conley pulled off his soiled kimono and laid it aside, then unwound his undergarment, and pulled it off his loins.

She was nude, her body badly bruised from where she had been beaten.

Taranaga stepped out of his slippers and entered the shower. Gloria followed him in, soaping his body, gently washing the dirt and grime from him.

He looked down at her as she worked. She had been very good. She had killed one man in the Englishman's hotel room, and had badly hurt the second man sent for her.

She was a tigress. She was beautiful. And it would be a shame that she would have to die this night.

The hotel clerk was gone when Briggs careened

down the stairs. The lobby was in semi-darkness, only the light from the buildings across the street providing any illumination.

The bar across the lobby was empty. The entire hotel was deathly still.

Briggs pulled up short just outside the stairway. The counter was to his left, the bar beyond it. Straight across were the front doors, and to the right, nothing but a blank wall.

Briggs stepped forward. Two small, compactly built men dressed in black pajamas stepped through the front door. One circled to the left, the other to the right.

For just a moment Briggs was nonplused. Both men were armed with long daggers. In addition, each carried a second weapon in his left hand: The one to the left carried a short length of stainless steel chain, with a three-sided blade on one end of it and a knurled handle at the other. The man to the right carried a long samurai sword.

Gloria had come here and Taranaga had sent his people after her. Now they had come for him.

He knew he had a number of options. He could turn, go back up to his room, and go out the window. He could try to talk his way out of the situation—although he doubted if that was a viable option. Or he could try to find a better weapon than his stiletto.

But why bother, he thought. He slipped the blade out of its sheath at the small of his back and grinned. Someone had been hurt up in his room. At this point, he had to believe it had been the girl. And that made him mad. He kept seeing the body of his mother lying in a bloody heap in their flat in Soho many years ago.

He dropped to a crouch and stepped forward, out into the middle of the lobby, directly between the two ninja warriors.

"Well, lads," he said softly. "It looks as if it's come time to teach you some manners. Especially how to treat a lady."

It was doubtful that either of the two men spoke English, but they understood the determined grin on Briggs's face and it made them just a bit more cautious.

Taranaga-san had told them that this one was very good, and would be difficult to kill cleanly.

Against both men, Briggs figured he had no chance. He was going to have to even the odds. Starting now.

He feinted left, toward the man with the chain weapon. The sword warrior started his charge, and Briggs spun on his heel, reversing his stiletto so that he had it loosely by the blade, and flipped it out with all of his might, the nine inches of steel burying itself in the ninja's chest.

Leaping backward as the ninja continued forward on his own momentum, Briggs reached out and snatched the sword from the man's dying grasp, then spun right, the chain-sword buzzing inches from his head.

"Hai, Hai, Hai," Briggs screamed as he leaped toward the ninja warrior, swinging the samurai sword with each lunge.

The ninja was very good, however, and managed to parry each thrust; and after the third, he kicked out with the side of his left foot, catching Briggs squarely in the hip and sending him sprawling.

The warrior was on him in a split second, swinging the deadly chain-sword, the three-sided blade biting deeply into the wooden floor barely an inch from Briggs's head.

Slamming his shoulder into the man's chest, Briggs shoved the warrior aside, but lost his grip on the samurai sword, which clattered to the floor. Before Briggs could recover it, the ninja slashed out with his dagger, opening a shallow cut in his side.

Briggs reared back, away from the second slash, catching the warrior's elbow with a perfectly timed karate chop.

The ninja dropped his dagger and leaped back, immediately dropping into the classic fighter's crouch.

Briggs's first instinct was to press the attack. But he was off balance, and he held his position, readying himself for the ninja's next move.

The warrior moved sideways, angling toward his dead companion, who still clutched a dagger even as Briggs's stiletto jutted from his chest.

Briggs circled the other way, keeping himself between the fallen warrior and the weapons. He grinned. The odds had been impossible before, they weren't so bad at the moment.

"It's all over, pal," Briggs said under his breath.

The ninja attacked, leaping high into the air and kicking out with both feet, one of them catching Briggs's left shoulder as he side-stepped.

The warrior came down, and Briggs spun in toward him, clubbing the back of his head with his hands tightly clasped in a short, effective weapon.

The ninja rolled twice, then started to get up, but Briggs was right on him and clipped the warrior on the jaw with his right heel.

The warrior's head bounced against the floor, and he lay still for just a moment or two, dazed. Briggs's side was on fire from his cracked rib, and from the cut, and his left shoulder was so numb that his left arm and hand were nearly useless.

He was hunched over, trying to catch his breath, when, incredibly, the ninja leaped to his feet and charged, his head down like a battering ram.

Briggs straightened up, side-stepped the charge, and as the man passed him, Briggs put everything he possessed into a perfectly swung right hook. It caught the smaller man squarely on the chin, lifting him bodily off the floor, his jaw breaking with an audible pop, and he crumpled in a heap, his hand inches from the samurai sword Briggs had dropped.

Briggs leaped on him, but the ninja did not move. The warrior's eyes were open; his head lolled at an impossible angle.

The ninja was dead. His jaw had broken, and so had his neck.

For several moments Briggs just stood there, looking down at both dead men. Finally, though, catching his breath, he pulled his stiletto from the body of the first ninja, wiped it on the man's black pajamas, then stumbled into the deserted bar.

He let his gaze travel around the barroom. There was no one here. They had all gone, knowing what was going to happen.

He ducked under the bar opening, and from the

shelves behind grabbed a bottle of bourbon. He opened it, took a deep drink, then pulled off his tattered, bloody shirt and poured some of the whiskey directly on his wound, the pain nearly causing him to faint.

He took another deep drink of the bourbon, the liquor hitting his stomach and rebounding like hot lead.

Carrying the bottle with him, he went back out into the bloody shambles of the lobby, then dragged himself up the stairs to his room.

With the lights out, had stripped off his sodden clothing and stepped into the shower, at first running the water as hot as he could stand it, his wound bleeding profusely, and then as cold as he could take it, forcing himself to remain under the spray until his head cleared.

Back in his room, he used the stiletto to cut several long strips of cloth from the bed sheets. One strip he folded over on itself and used as a pad; the other strips he used to tie the pad around the wound in his side, binding it tightly to hold his cracked rib in place as well.

He got dressed in clean khakis and soft leather boots, then lit himself a cigarette, inhaling deeply, the smoke making him light-headed for the first few seconds. He took another deep drink of the bourbon, then tossed the bottle aside.

Taranaga's ninja warriors were very good. Much better than he had suspected they would be. In fact, he was worried at the moment. He had barely managed to hold his own with two of them. Most likely Taranaga's place was crawling with the men. Impossible to beat—at least, using ordinary means.

But Gloria was there. Taranaga had sent his people here to bring her back. Christ. God only knew what he was doing to the girl at the moment.

And God only knew what was happening out at the base. Whatever it was, it certainly was not pleasant.

It bothered him, though, that he knew where his duty lay. And it was not in the direction of Taranaga's private secretary.

Briggs had just turned away from the window when a tremendous explosion rocked the entire hotel, the floor under his feet tilting crazily inward, flames shooting up from outside, window glass spraying everywhere.

Gloria helped Taranaga out of the shower, up two wooden-slat steps, and down into the hot, fragrant water of a large circular tub.

Her heart was nearly beating out of her chest. Taranaga could feel it in the way she shivered as she took his arm and helped him down. It heightened his pleasure, knowing that she was frightened, and knowing that she would die so very soon.

Behind him, on the shelf over the rim of the tub, were a half-dozen potted plants. Behind one of them was a long, deadly, ceremonial dagger. As Gloria kneaded the muscles of his back, he smiled, and reached behind the plants to touch it. The cool steel felt comforting to his fingers.

He turned and motioned for her to stand on the step. She slowly turned, offering her entire body for his approval.

He reached out and tenderly slapped her buttocks. She looked back, in surprise. He had never been this gentle with her. Never. And it served to heighten her fear of what would happen to her.

When she had been brought back to the compound, she had groveled in the dust at his feet. But he had ignored her. At that moment his anger had been too uncontained to do any justice to his true feelings toward her.

He had saved her for just this moment, when he was in control.

She stepped back into the water, the soft, light hair of her pubis under the water, her breasts several inches above the warm surface.

Taranaga reached out and caressed her perfectly formed breasts. Despite her fear and obvious revulsion of him, her nipples hardened. He reached up and ran his fingertip across her lips.

"Do not turn away," he said, when she started to turn her head.

She looked back at him. Her chest rose and fell, her nostrils flared, and her eyes were wide.

Taranaga could feel himself responding to the deliciousness of the moment. It was as if this entire scene, including all of its emotions, were set down in an exquisitely done watercolor. He could see his anger and her fear so crystally clear; so sharply defined.

"Let me go from here," she said ever so softly.

"What?"

"Please, Taranaga-san. Let me go from here. My father will do as you say. You are done with me, in any case. There is no longer a need for me here."

Taranaga smiled indulgently. How marvelous, he thought. The bitch pleads. "How would you leave?" he asked.

"On the delivery airplane. When it comes next I would go. There would be no bother to you."

"How would you leave?" he asked again.

She did not understand what he was saying, and he could see in her eyes that she desperately wanted to understand. She desperately wanted to have some hope.

"What would you use for money, my child? You are penniless."

"My father . . . my father has money. He would pay you."

Taranaga smiled. "Your father will be dead within the week, child. There is no hope for him."

She gasped.

"Or for you," Taranaga said.

"I will do anything for you. Anything you want of me. Only please, I beg of you, please let me go from here."

Taranaga drew the girl to him, and kissed her deeply on the lips. When they parted there were tears in her eyes.

He pulled her close again, and gently kissed her breasts; one at a time, running his tongue around her hardened nipples; teasing her with his teeth, playing a game with her, so that it made her shiver despite the warmth of the water.

His hands went below the water to her thighs. She flinched, but he parted them, and his fingers sought and found the delicate rose-petal opening. She shivered harder.

Taranaga was ready. He could feel himself near the bursting point. Unusual for him, he thought. But delicious.

Again, he made her climb out of the water; only now she straddled his chest, and he bent forward and kissed her lovely, moist mound, her hands going involuntarily to his head, holding him, guiding him. They had done this before. Often. But never with so much tenderness; never before with so much feeling.

Taranaga pulled back, and helped her slide down into the water. She was flushed, but the anger and disgust were still there behind her eyes.

"I will let you go," he said softly. "You will be happy. It will be away from here, from me."

"Yes?" she said, not daring to hope.

"Yes," he said with a smile. "But there is one last thing you must do for me. You have done it before, often. It is our little game."

"Yes?" she said.

He was hard. He guided her lower, so that the water was at her chin. "Now," he said.

Gently, he shoved her head under the water. She knew exactly what he wanted, and with only his guidance, she pulled herself down, taking his entire length in her mouth and working back and forth.

He put his hands on the back of her head, holding her down, at first helping her back and forth, but then settling back, closing his eyes and holding himself in check.

She would have to remain there until he came. It was a little game of their's that showed his power over her. In the past, though, he had never directed her there until he was on the verge.

He had wanted to kill her with the dagger. It had been his father's. But this way was better. This way was much better—and would be supreme if he could time his ejaculation with her last conscious moment. How wondrous.

She began to struggle, but in the position she was in between his legs, with his hands on her head, he was much stronger than her.

He clamped his old knees against her head. He could feel himself nearly coming. She was thrashing around heavily now. She knew she was going to die . . .

Suddenly there was an excruciating, unbelievable, pain there.

Taranaga reared back screaming, his knees coming apart, his hands shoving Gloria away as he grabbed himself, the bath water turning bright red.

Gloria came up, gasping, one inch of the end of his bitten-through penis still in her mouth.

Eleven

The lights were out, and Briggs lay in a crumpled heap against the corridor wall, the entire top floor of the hotel tilted at a crazy angle. The air was thick with smoke, and it was already becoming uncomfortably hot.

Briggs rolled over and managed to get to his hands and knees, pushing up against the wall that was below him now.

Flames ate at the outer wall, around the window that had overlooked the drainage ditch outside but that now pointed up at the night sky.

Fumbling around in the dark, he finally managed to find the door from his room. He yanked it open, pulling it up and around, and then half-stumbled, half-fell, into the corridor.

The stairs were gone. A huge, gaping hole showing flames and smoke defined the end of the corridor. Very soon the entire hotel would be a blazing inferno in which absolutely nothing could live.

But he was still groggy. The battering he had taken, the lack of food and proper sleep, the booze — and now the intense smoke he was pulling into the lungs — tended to distort everything in his perception.

It took him the longest time just to understand that he was in mortal danger, and that he could not simply walk to the end of the hall and go down the stairs, cross the lobby, and step out into the cool street.

Street! The single word as a concept congealed in his mind.

Street! he said over and over again.

He got up, and rolled against the far corridor wall. He fumbled with his hands and fingers, finally finding a doorknob, which he twisted. But the door would not open. It was locked!

Briggs managed to pull back, climbing to the high side of the corridor, and then he pushed himself off the high wall, slamming into the door with all of his might, the fleeting thought crossing his mind that if the room he was about to crash into was filled with flames, he would be a dead man.

He hit the door, the pain jolting through his body, and the thin wood splintered as the safety chain gave way. He fell inside, into the springs of the big bed that was upside down against the outer wall.

The room was so thick with smoke that Briggs could not see anything but the flickering red flames around him.

He could not breathe; he could not think; and for several awful seconds he could not move — he was held fast by the jagged edges of the bedsprings, like the clutching, sharp claws of some insensitive monster.

He tore his body away from the springs and pulled the bed up away from the outer wall. Lifting it up with sheer brute strength, so that he could see the open window it had covered, he leaped forward, pushing it through the glass and following it out into the air fifteen feet above the dusty, littered street.

He hit hard, the wind driven out of him. For a long time — a seeming eternity — he lay there, not really aware of anything.

Finally, though, he became vaguely conscious that something malevolent loomed over him, and he focused his eyes.

The front wall of the hotel, furiously on fire now, was roasting him like the upper element in a broiling oven, and threatened to fall down on him at any moment.

Briggs scrambled up the street on his hands and knees for ten yards, then managed to get to his feet and race the rest of the way away from the burning hotel, finally coming to a halt a hundred yards away.

Three dozen townspeople stood blocking the street. Most of them carried bats or long, stout sticks. A few of them held broken bottles, the jagged edges blood-red in the light from the burning hotel.

"Traitor," someone shouted.

"*Traitor*," the entire group chanted.

Briggs stumbled backward a few steps. Taranaga had the entire town brainwashed. Christ!

Briggs looked over his shoulder. The front wall of the hotel had sagged even farther over the street. It would collapse at any moment, cutting off any means of escape from what was turning out to be a very ugly situation. Fighting a pair of highly trained ninja killers was one thing. Going up against an angry mob, armed with bottles and clubs, was a totally different matter, and from which Briggs could not possibly emerge unscathed.

The crowd started forward, chanting: "Traitor! Traitor!"

Briggs spun on his heel and raced back up the street, the crowd bolting after him, bottles and clubs raining down around him.

A large section of the hotel's front wall collapsed in the street, flames and sparks rising high into the night sky. More of the hotel was ready to fall when Briggs reached it, but without hesitation he dodged around the downed section, and raced toward safety on the other side.

A roar rose from the crowd behind him. He spun around. The townspeople had stopped at the far side of the hotel. Even as he watched, the hotel front collapsed in a huge, flaming heap, driving him farther down the now-deserted street.

His jeep was beneath the pile of burning rubble. Its fuel tank exploded, spreading more flames to some of the other buildings in the block.

Soon the entire downtown would be on fire. But sooner than that, the townspeople who had been after his blood would be coming around the block. And this time he'd not be able to duck under some burning building to escape so easily.

At the end of the block Briggs stopped, trying to decide if he should make a run for the docks, where he might be able to find a boat, or back up into the hills that led on the other side to the north beach.

Diagonally across the street, however, he spotted a low, cement-block building, behind which rose a tower with a small transmission dish atop it. The phone company.

Briggs could hear the sounds of the angry crowd coming past the rear of the main street buildings. They'd be around the corner at any second.

He raced across the street. The front door of the stoutly built exchange was locked, but he managed to open it with his stiletto.

He was just slipping into the building and closing the door when the first of the mob came around the corner. Their attention was directed back toward the hotel, otherwise they would have spotted him.

For a minute or so Briggs remained by the door, which he held open a crack, watching the antics of the mob. They had gone crazy. Not able to find Briggs, they were breaking windows, tearing doors off, and even toppling two light poles. They were on a rampage.

Briggs closed the door the rest of the way, making sure that the lock caught, and then he flipped on a light in the windowless room.

There was a small counter just inside the main door, and Briggs hefted a stout metal chair over it, wedging the doorknob. He went into the main room, which was filled with automatic switching and telephone transmission equipment.

A desk in one corner held a telephone. He went to it, his hand reaching out for the instrument. But then he looked up.

If he picked up the telephone, there was a very

good chance that Taranaga would know who it was. And if that was the case, he would also know where Briggs was, and would send instructions to the mob.

Briggs went around to the back of the equipment racks, finding the service door to the rear of the building. He carefully opened the door and looked outside. From here he could see the flames rising into the sky from the burning hotel, and although he could still hear the crowd, he could see no one.

He ducked back into the equipment room, and at the desk hesitated only a moment longer before he picked up the telephone.

The instrument was not dead; he could hear the hollowness of the line—but there was no dial tone.

He jiggled the button, cutting the circuit, but there was still no dial tone.

Turning around, Briggs hung up the telephone and stepped across the narrow aisle to the equipment. Lights were lit. Dials read voltages and amperages. But for some reason the system was not working for him.

It could have been something as simple as a flipped switch somewhere or a minor malfunction. But it would take a trained technician to figure it out, although Briggs had no doubt that, given time, he could work it out himself.

There was no time tonight, though. He went again to the rear door and looked outside. There was still no sign of the mob, although he could hear them screaming and shouting, and he could hear the sounds of breaking glass. Taranaga's people would be hitting the base tonight. And God only knew what was happening to Gloria at this moment.

He looked back at the telephone on the desk, then shook his head. There simply wasn't the time. They were on their own on this one. By morning, when they might be able to get back down here with a technician, it would be over one way or the other.

He had been in tighter spots, he figured. But he resolved never to underestimate these people again.

Slipping out the back door of the telephone exchange, Briggs kept low as he raced across the yard to the fence around the transmission tower. There, he surveyed his prospects.

One way, across the side road, the main street ran up to the burning hotel, where there were still dozens of townspeople on the rampage. The other way, across the dirt road and up about a hundred yards, was the shipping company's depot and storage yard. If there'd be any sort of transportation left here in town, Briggs figured it'd be there.

He made his way around to the far side of the tower, where he was out of sight from the crowd, then ducked into the low underbrush and trees.

Within five minutes he had made it to a point just across from the depot. He raced quickly across the dirt road, not sure at all if anyone from the mob had spotted him, and scrambled over the low, wire-mesh fence into the storage yard.

Two metal sheds, one of them with windows, were set off to one side of the main gate. Farther back into the yard, which was stacked with everything from lumber to concrete blocks and sheet metal to canned goods, Briggs spotted what he had come looking for, and headed directly across the yard to it.

Parked beside the fuel pumps was a large, antiquated dump truck with a split wind screen that opened in the front, and open sides—no doors.

He jumped up on the running board and looked inside. There was no key. The ignition was simply a toggle switch on the dash, with a button for a starter.

He got behind the wheel, made sure he knew how to work the shift and the emergency brake, then flipped the toggle switch. There was no fuel gauge. He hoped for the best. He pushed the starter button and the old motor weakly turned over; he gave it gas. It coughed, and finally started with a huge roar.

The mob would have heard the truck starting. They'd know who it was. There was no time now for mistakes.

Briggs jammed the truck into gear and pulled away from the pumps. The ancient vehicle bucked and heaved, but it accelerated, and he managed to shift it into second—just before he hit the main gate and then he was crashing through, and turning down the dirt road toward the downtown.

The mob had come around the corner and they raced up the street toward him. Briggs pressed the accelerator pedal to the floor, the old truck shuddering with the unaccustomed beating it was getting.

He shifted into third, and he was flashing by the people who parted for him, bottles and clubs and rocks smashing into the windscreen—starring it.

One man tried to leap up on the running board, but Briggs swerved the truck sharply to the right, and then back again. The man lost his grip, and with a sharply punctuated scream he fell beneath the big front wheels.

Briggs drove across the main street down to the

road that went along the waterfront, then angled a few blocks later up to the main highway leading out of town, the sounds of the crowd and the smell of the burning hotel fading, the fresh air wonderful.

As he drove, his pounding heart started settling down, and his head began to clear, but his body felt battered. He was in desperate need of rest and food, but he knew that he would get none of that this night. If he was still alive in time for breakfast, he figured he would celebrate.

The ancient truck made it to the turnoff to the base, and Briggs slowed down and stopped. He turned off the engine, and got out of the truck, cocking his head so that he could better hear.

But the night was silent except for the birds and the insects in the trees and brush. If the base was coming under attack now, it was being done silently.

There were no sounds of gunshots, no screams, no flames to light the night sky. Nothing.

He looked up the road toward Taranaga's compound. It was very possible that Gloria was dead by now. There had been a lot of blood in his room. And it was more likely that Gloria had been hurt than the ninja who had come for her.

Evidently he had misjudged her. She had apparently submitted to Taranaga's sexual perversions for some compelling reason, some blackmail or hold he evidently had over her.

Christ, it made him almost see red. He kept thinking about his mother's death. And he thought about Sylvia Hume, whom he loved against all the odds. She was British aristocracy. He was Irish-Soho scum. She was a lady; he was a hired thug . . . a killer.

Briggs jumped back into the truck, started the wheezing engine again, and crashed through the gears on his way up the road to Taranaga's compound. The base was not under attack. And if it was, there were grown men there who could and would defend themselves. They could wait for one more fighting man. Gloria might not be able to.

Taranaga, in a finely honed rage, lay on his back in the dispensary, his legs spread, while his medic finished stitching the roughly severed end of his penis. The last drops of a pint of blood, suspended on a holder, were flowing into the old man's veins.

The medic had wanted to give Taragana a massive painkiller, but the old man had refused, accepting only a local anesthetic.

A short catheter tube had been sewn into the urethra and extended an inch or so beyond the bandages, so that Taranaga would be able to urinate without contaminating the wound.

"You were lucky, Taranaga-san," the medic said conversationally. He was an old man, who had seen a lot and was not frightened of his boss. "You could easily have bled to death."

"Shut up, old man," Taranaga snapped.

The doctor looked up and shook his head. "You will not tell me how this has happened. But it appears to me that it was an animal bite."

"Shut up," Taranaga screamed.

The old man was unperturbed. He finished the stitching and the bandaging. They were alone in the dispensary. Taranaga had, of course, insisted on it.

"I must know, Taranaga-san. If it was an animal, then we may have to give you rabies vaccinations. Otherwise, you might die."

Taranaga, shaking now, rose. He looked down at himself. "Are you finished?"

"Yes, I am," the medic said.

Taranaga ripped the blood-bag tube out of his arm and flung it aside. He got very painfully to his feet, swaying there for a minute. The medic tried to help him, but Taranaga brushed the man's hands away.

Finally, he tottered across the room to where his fresh things had been brought in. He turned and looked back at the doctor, who was bent over now, picking up the blood transfusion bag and tube that had been knocked to the floor.

Taranaga slipped his ceremonial dagger from its sheath by his clothing, and holding it behind him, came back to where the medic was still bent over.

Taranaga had to walk bowlegged because of his wound, and the pain was excruciating, but he did not feel it now. The medic had dared question him!

The medic looked up, and reading murder in Taranaga's eyes started to cry out, but Taranaga swung the dagger around and brought it down, burying it in the man's shoulder between the base of his neck and his collarbone, severing several major arteries.

Taranaga viciously jerked the razor-sharp blade left and right, the steel deflecting off the bones and cartilage, severing, among other things, the medic's windpipe.

The old man thrashed around for a moment or two

longer, then sank down on the floor, dead.

"Death to traitors," Taranaga said softly.

He had never lost his grip on the dagger. He took it now to the sink and methodically washed it, and then sponged himself off.

When he was finished, he calmly dressed in his clean clothing, careful not to step in any of the blood that had splattered across the small dispensary from the medic's struggles.

Then he hobbled to the door, and stepped outside. Nojima Tosu, his new lieutenant, was waiting for him.

The man bowed. Taranaga returned the bow, painfully, then together they went across the compound to the main house, where the staff was respectfully gathered.

There had been a lot of talk in the past hour since Taranaga had brought himself to the dispensary and had begun issuing orders. But each of his staff well understood that should a single word of their talk get back to Taranaga-san, they would all surely die this extraordinary night.

"One million American dollars, and transport to any city on the earth, for the man or woman who brings me Gloria Conley alive and unhurt," Taranaga said, very softly.

Three of the staffers gasped involuntarily. So the rumors had been true!

Taranaga ignored the outburst. "One million dollars and transport anywhere on earth for the man or woman who brings me the interloper who calls himself Blake, unharmed."

"But Taranaga-san, is not the man called Blake

dead by now in the city?" Tosu asked.

"Do not underestimate this man," Taranaga said. He looked up, almost as if he were sniffing the air. "No," he said, half to himself, "I think he is still alive."

Twelve

Briggs stood beside the silent truck, listening to the night sounds. He was less than a half mile below Taranaga's compound, but he was not able to see or hear a thing, except the night jungle sounds and the bulk of the dormant volcano looming above.

His urge all along had been to go crashing into the compound, grab Taranaga, and kill him. Somehow he would find Gloria, and they'd get out of there, back to the base.

This close, however, he had begun to think it out. Even if he got to Taranaga, the old man would be defended. By his ninja warriors, no doubt. If the rest of them were half as good as the two back in the hotel lobby, Briggs knew he would not have a chance. At least not using normal combat techniques.

Briggs managed to grin. Hit and run, wasn't that what the Vietcong had taught them?.

He got back in the truck, started it, and headed up

the hill, gathering speed as he went, the old truck grinding and clanking, threatening to fall apart at any moment.

"Come on," Briggs said softly under his breath. "Just a little more."

He had it in fourth gear and was doing better than thirty miles per hour when he came around the last curve before the main gate to the compound. He slammed the accelerator pedal to the floor, and ducked down so that his eyes were just above the level of the wind screen.

He caught the impression of several men scrambling out of the way, and then he hit the gate, slamming it off its hinges. He flashed past the gatehouse, the guards coming after him in a dead run.

Only a few lights were showing in the compound, although most of the cars were still there. No one was in sight.

Briggs straightened up, aiming the truck toward the back bumpers of the dozen cars and jeeps parked in a row.

He braced himself for the collision, and then he was slamming and bouncing off the backs of the other vehicles, the heavy truck shoving them in jumbled heaps on top of each other.

Glass flew everywhere, and there was a long flash behind him as spraying gasoline from a ruptured fuel tank hit one of the outdoor lanterns. A second later a huge explosion lit the night sky, and then another and a third shattered the jungle silence.

Briggs aimed the big truck up toward Taranaga's rice-paper house, downshifting to third just before he hit the veranda where the party had been held, bouncing up and through the front of the house, crushing the furniture and shoving a grand piano through the far wall.

The truck had come to a halt, but the engine had not stalled. Someone was shooting at the truck, so he rammed it into reverse and backed out, slamming across the veranda, and into the compound again.

The guards from the main gate had come up into the clearing, and they were firing automatic rifles. But they were hitting nowhere near the cab. A part of Briggs's brain registered that fact. They wanted him alive.

He slammed the truck into first, and swung it around, heading directly for the four men firing at him. It was then he realized that the back end of the truck was on fire.

Flames shot out from beneath the undercarriage. As soon as the fuel tank — which was directly behind the seats — heated up enough, there would be a tremendous explosion.

Briggs pulled the throttle all the way out to its stop, the engine racing suddenly as he swung the big truck around and aimed it back at the main house.

The guards were unloading their automatic weapons on him now, but they were still not aiming toward the cab.

Twenty-five yards away from the house, the flames from beneath the truck rising up and licking at the cab, Briggs rolled out from behind the steering wheel and leaped from the cab.

At that moment the front right tire blew, and the truck swerved sharply, turning over as Briggs hit the dust, and going up in a huge ball of flame well short of the main house, as Briggs rolled three painful times.

For a long moment Briggs lay there on his side trying to catch his breath, a sharp pain hitting at him each time he breathed.

Then he rolled over in time to look up into the barrels of four automatic rifles, and six of the other house staff with raised clubs.

Taranaga wanted him. Taranaga now had him. If nothing else, Briggs figured he'd finally find out just why the Japanese madman so desperately wanted the British off this island.

He slowly sat up, keeping his hands in clear view. They had been careful not to hurt him so far, but he did not want to tempt providence any farther than he already had.

"Hai," one of the guards snapped, motioning with his rifle for Briggs to get to his feet.

Briggs got up, his side on fire, his one arm nearly useless for the moment. The guards backed off, and the same one motioned for him to head up to the main house.

Behind them the long line of cars was burning furiously, and off to the right, flames shot high up into the night sky from the truck. Ahead, the entire front of the main house was collapsed, and in shambles.

Briggs was directed through a side gate, all but two of his guards remaining behind. But four other armed men, ninja in black pajamas, were waiting inside for him.

He went down a broad corridor, grass mats on the

floor, and outside to Taranaga's private rock garden. Taranaga himself was seated on a pile of cushions in the corner. He looked pale, as if he were in some pain.

Briggs approached, but the ninja guards looped a coil of line around his neck and they pulled him up short, ten feet away.

Taranaga just looked at him, pure, venomous hate radiating from every pore of his body.

Briggs grinned. "Sorry to barge in like this, but—"

Taranaga nodded ever so slightly, and the ninja pulled Briggs down to the floor by the line around his neck, and kicked and slammed him with their feet and fists.

They jumped back as quickly as they had attacked, and let him slowly recover. He finally sat up, the house spinning around him, the floor threatening to come up to his face.

"Before this night is finished, you will be pleased to provide me with two small bits of information," Taranaga said. His voice was still a little shaky.

It was obvious to Briggs, even in his battered condition, that something was wrong with the old Japanese. The old man sat with his legs spread, and he held himself as if he were in pain.

"I'll trade you," Briggs said. His jaw felt almost as if it were dislocated. It was very difficult to speak clearly.

"Yes?" Taranaga asked. His eyes were shiny.

Briggs grinned. "You tell me what happened to you, and I'll tell you—"

Something very hard, like a club, slammed into Briggs's back, sending him sprawling forward, the line around his neck pulling him up short, cutting his wind off.

He was dizzy, but he tried to straighten up to relieve the pressure from the cord. Something was holding him forward. Something was pushing him harder against the cord around his neck. He dimly understood it was a foot. They were going to strangle him to death now, and he did not have the strength to prevent it.

He rolled his eyes, just managing to see Taranaga. He curled his lips up in a macabre smile. If this was it, then so be it. But he wasn't going to give the son of a bitch any satisfaction.

Taranaga made a slight motion with his right hand, and the pressure was released from Briggs's back. He was pulled back, the strain off the cord. He was seeing spots before his eyes, and there was a terrible rushing in his ears.

Briggs had to make a real effort to keep himself erect, to keep himself from falling over. Slowly, the anger was continuing to build inside of him. Taranaga was going to pay for this.

"Two things I wish to know," Taranaga's hateful voice came to him through the haze.

Briggs looked up. He managed to grin.

"The first is your real name, and the second is who sent you here."

Briggs tried to croak out a reply, but his throat constricted in pain, and nothing came out. He lowered his head a moment, trying to swallow, trying to open his windpipe so that he could breathe. Gradually, the muscles of his bruised throat relaxed, and he could draw in a breath. He looked up again.

"Perhaps you will not talk to me just yet, but you will," Taranaga said. "I will say, though, that I do admire your strength and your courage. Although I can only pity your stupidity."

Briggs did not try to talk. He just stared into Taranaga's eyes. Whatever had happened to the old man, and Briggs was sure something had, he sincerely hoped that it hurt like hell.

At least a half dozen ninja and several dozen other Japanese all suddenly were crowded around where Briggs was crouched. They all bowed deeply to Taranaga.

One of them—the one who had spoken to Briggs back at the hotel—stepped forward.

Taranaga addressed him. "It is time now to eliminate the British presence on this island. It is time to eradicate the spy-satellite receiving station. Are you ready to do this thing for me?"

"Yes, Taranaga-san."

"Are you ready to send them back into the sea from whence they came?"

"Yes, Taranaga-san."

"Death to the traitors," Taranaga said.

"Death to traitors," the entire group screamed.

Steve Graves had absolutely no doubt in his mind that Briggs was right, and that there would be another attack this night. It was only a question of exactly when and in what manner the attack would come.

He wasn't cut out for this. He had been a desk man with the service—at least for most of his career.

He had been in the field, of course. Every career officer with the SIS who expected to be promoted beyond the grade of junior analyst had to do his time in the field.

But his duty stations had been places such as Lisbon, Rome, and even Washington, D.C., where he'd been a liaison officer with the CIA.

This was to have been his last field duty before being kicked upstairs to work only a few echelons below Hope-Turner himself.

Graves had all the proper credentials for taking over the top spot someday. He had gone to the correct prep school, the proper university — Oxford was still considered tops — and had done his stint in the Royal Air Force.

He had arranged this assignment himself, actually, as a sort of sinecure for service well met. A final eighteen months in the bush, eating coconut, and drinking bad beer. Not so bad, really, considering what was waiting back in London.

From the window of his second-floor barracks room he could see across most of the compound, out toward the main gate in one direction, and the cliffs and ocean in the other. It was very dark across the base. They had turned out all the lights. It had been Webb's idea, actually, and a damned fine one at that.

Not only had they turned out all the lights across the base, they had positioned them and spotlights at strategic points around the perimeter of the base. When the attack came, the lights would suddenly be switched on, not only blinding the attackers, but making them stand out in high relief; they'd be sitting ducks.

Someone knocked on his door.

"Come," he said, turning away from the window.

The door opened and one of the engineers struck his head in. "They want you at the main gate, sir," he said.

"What is it?"

"It's that woman—Gloria Conley—who was here earlier. She's back, sir. Says she wants in."

Graves started to shake his head, but then he thought better of it. "What did Mr. Webb have to say?"

"We can't find him, sir."

"Did the woman say what she wanted, other than in?"

"Yes, sir. Said she had some valuable information for us. About the attack that's coming tonight."

Graves hated to make decisions on his own; after all, he wasn't in charge of this base. And if they had listened to him in the first place, Bower would never have gone off to Taranaga's. And they would have called the Royal Marines long ago.

But, hell—as it stood, Webb was only a construction supervisor, after all, and O'Meara was not here.

He grabbed his automatic rifle from where it had been laying on his bed. "I'll come down to talk to her myself," he said.

"Yes, sir," the engineer said. "I'll be getting back to work, then."

"What are you doing?"

"We're trying to jerry-rig a decent antenna to go with one of our emergency locator transmitters from the air/sea rescue pack."

"Good luck," Graves said, and he really meant it.

This island had been strange to him from the moment he had arrived here. There had been nothing but death and destruction on this base. Station death, he had been calling it in his private operational log. Someday, when it was time to retire and to write his memoirs, he'd need the notes.

He followed the young engineer downstairs and outside. The engineer went back over to one of the supply buildings, and Graves jumped in his jeep and headed down to the main gate.

The more Graves thought about it, the more he was amazed at himself. Gloria Conley was Taranaga's secretary. Why hadn't she been questioned before? O'Meara apparently thought she was worth the effort. He had made it quite clear that he wanted her in if she returned.

There had been no word from him since he had stormed off into town. But Graves had a feeling that O'Meara was one man who could take care of himself.

The headlights of Graves's jeep illuminated the main gate, but he switched them off as he pulled up.

Two of the gate guards came out, and challenged him. He stood away from the jeep. They shone a light on his face, so that they could make sure who it was.

"She's just in here, Mr. Graves," one of them said.

Graves followed the man into the small guard hut. Gloria Conley, blood down her face and neck and chest, dressed only in the rags of what once had been a spotlessly white kimono, lay back in the shack's only chair. Her eyes were fluttering. The kimono had fallen open, exposing one of her lovely breasts and most of her thighs. The sight practically took Graves's breath away. No wonder O'Meara thought so much of her. She was beautiful.

"Miss Conley?" Graves said.

Gloria snapped awake, and then sat up. "Are you Graves? The SIS?"

Her knowledge took his breath away too. "I'm Steve Graves," he said cautiously.

She just sat there, not bothering to cover herself. It bothered Graves.

"It is the man who calls himself Rupert Blake. Is he here?"

"No, he's not. He went back into town," Graves said. "But he told us that if you were to come back here—"

She jumped up, the kimono falling all the way open, fully exposing her.

"Are you sure he went back into town?" she screeched.

Graves swallowed hard. Christ, she had one hell of a body! He turned. The two gate guards stood in the doorway, open-mouthed. "Get the hell back to your positions," he said.

"Ah . . . yes, sir," they said, practically stumbling over each other getting out.

Graves turned back. "No, Miss Conley, I'm not sure he went back into town. But when he left he said that's where he was headed. Now could you please cover yourself."

Gloria looked down at her own nakedness, and nonchalantly pulled the kimono closed.

Christ, she didn't even give a damn! Graves figured she had been around the Japanese too long.

"Are you hurt, miss?" he asked.

"No, no," she mumbled, brushing at the blood down her front.

"They told me that you apparently have some information about this base being attacked?"

"Taranaga is insane. He's doing this. It's been him all along."

"Taranaga has been doing what?" Graves asked, very careful now. He wanted to make absolutely certain he understood her perfectly. He wanted to make no mistakes now.

"Killing your people, you fool!" she screeched. "Attacking this base. Causing all your accidents."

"Why?"

"I don't know . . . for sure. But before this night is over, he intends to overrun this base. There will be no one left alive."

"With only villagers . . . ?"

"No, he has brought in ninja warriors from Japan. They have been gathering one or two at a time for months now. He has enough to kill you all."

"But why?" Graves asked. This was the part that none of them could understand. "He can't get away with it."

"He has already. No one will believe a multi-billionaire could or would do something like this. When it is over he will hide all of the evidence. No one will ever know."

"There will be an investigation."

"He will control it. He has his people — his spies — everywhere. Don't you see the danger you are in?"

"Why are you here like this?"

She shook her head. She was obviously all in.

Graves looked out the window, through the main gate toward the road. "Where is your car?" he asked.

"I walked here. There was no time for a car. This is all so useless. Don't you see, this base will come under attack. Blake knows about it." She looked away. Then she jumped, hearing something. "He's in town. Taranaga will kill him. He'll kill us all."

Then Graves heard it. Someone chanting. At least that's what it sounded like. A great many people chanting something over and over. There! Toward the highway.

"It's them!" Gloria screamed, shrinking back. "Oh Jesus . . . Jesus. It's them. They've come for us. We're all going to die now!"

Thirteen

They had staked Briggs out so that he lay leaning forward, astraddle a woven cane chair. Two of Taranaga's house staff, wiry older men with knots for muscles, were there. Taranaga himself had not moved from his position among all the pillows.

Briggs was placed so that he could face the old man. He noticed that some blood had seeped onto the crotch of Taranaga's immaculately clean white outfit.

He had some sort of injury there. Something recent, enough to bleed, and to cause him, apparently, a great deal of pain.

On a signal from Taranaga the two housemen came forward, and with their razor-sharp ceremonial daggers cut the clothing away from Briggs, leaving him nude, firmly tied to the chair.

"In some respects, I hope that you will be very strong, Mr. Blake. I hope that you will meet your pain stoically, so that it can go on for a very long time," Taranaga said.

He made another slight motion, and the two men set a pan of some clear liquid on the floor between Briggs's legs. Briggs's testicles shrank, and his gut turned over. He knew damned well what the bastard was planning.

"In the end, however, you will talk to me, Mr. Blake," Taranaga said. He smiled.

Briggs heaved himself over and nearly fell, except that one of the men grabbed him and roughly shoved him back in place.

"Ah, I can see that you have an idea what it will be. Very simple, is it not? But very effective," Taranaga said. He again made a motion.

One of the men held Briggs firmly in place while the second lit the alcohol in the pan. The flames rose up, and Briggs could immediately feel the gentle heat on his crotch.

Taranaga poured himself a small glass of wine and sipped it, his eyes never leaving Briggs's.

"I will not ask you the two questions again, Mr. Blake. When you are ready to speak to me, I will listen. At that time I will decide whether I shall kill you at that moment, or prolong your miserable life so that you may die beside Miss Conley."

She had run off! the thought crossed Briggs's mind. The heat was beginning to build to an uncomfortable level beneath him. He tried to squirm out of the way, but his ropes held, and the two men kept his chair firmly in place.

"So it was Gloria who did that damage to you," Briggs said, taking a shot. He was beginning to sweat.

Taranaga sat forward so fast that some of his wine spilled, and his face grimaced in pain. "More," he screamed.

One of the two did something beneath Briggs, and suddenly the heat was unbearable on Briggs's testicles and anus, and he screamed involuntarily.

The pain seemed to go on forever before it finally began to subside, before the sharpness went out of it and it became somewhat easier to bear.

Taranaga held himself rigid. But his eyes were very wide, very bright.

Briggs shook his head. "Whatever she did to you, I sincerely hope it hurts . . . and I hope the hurt continues to—"

The pain struck at Briggs again, his entire insides binding in terrible knots all the way up into his armpits. Anything would be easier to bear than this, the dim, fleeting thought crossed his mind, and another ragged scream was torn against his will from deep inside his chest.

It took much longer this time for the pain to dull by even the slightest degree. His stomach was heaving, and he finally vomited. He could smell the odor of cooking flesh. It nauseated him even more, and he continued to heave long after there was nothing left in his stomach.

After a while he was able to pull deep draughts of air into his lungs, his stomach settling by degrees, but the pain at his crotch showed no sign of lessening.

Intellectually, Briggs suspected that he had been

damaged a lot less than his feelings told him he had. Yet it was hard to accept that he would not be damaged permanently.

All he could think about was Taranaga. He wanted desperately to get his hands on the man. He looked up, but his eyes did not seem to want to focus, although he could see it was Taranaga sitting there. The man was saying something, but the words were not intelligible either.

"You bastard," he heard his own croak from a long way off.

One of the housemen was suddenly in front of Briggs. He snapped something in his fingers, and waved it beneath Briggs's nose. Ammonia! Smelling salts!

The sharp odor rebounded inside Briggs's skull, and his vision and hearing instantly cleared, although he was still very weak, and light-headed.

"That's better," Taranaga said. "Do you have something to say to me?"

"Yes . . ." Briggs croaked. "Yes."

"Speak up. I can't hear you!" Taranaga demanded.

"Yes!" Briggs whispered. He hung his head, and closed his eyes. He could hear fabric rustling. Someone approached. Briggs looked up into Taranaga's face. One of the housemen was helping him stand.

"What is it?" Taranaga said, his ancient, lined face eager.

Briggs grinned. "Fuck you," he said, and with the little moisture he had been able to collect in his mouth, he spit on the man's face.

Taranaga reared back in rage. "You will die!" he screamed. "You will die so slowly that you will beg to be killed mercifully."

Briggs made his eyes flutter, and he let his head fall forward, as if he had passed out again, as he began to work on the rope that held his left wrist in place against a lower rung of the chair. It was loose.

A large crowd of townspeople came up the dirt road to the main gate. They were armed with clubs and bottles and rocks.

Graves had stepped out of the guardshack. The two guards had their weapons at the ready. "Hold it a moment," Graves said softly.

"Sir?" one of them asked uncertainly.

Gloria Conley had come to the open door. She looked out at the approaching crowd. She too seemed uncertain.

"Are these Taranaga's people?" Graves asked her.

She shook her head. "I don't know."

"They look like people from the town to me," Graves said. "Are they working for Taranaga?"

"Some of them are," Gloria said. "I don't know."

Graves looked up toward the base. Webb had used some of the locals from time to time to help with the construction. Or at least he had at the beginning. If anyone on the base would know the townspeople's mood, he would. Yet they were here, angry, wanting to attack. Why?

"Hold them here," Graves said to the guards. He led Gloria back to the jeep and helped her in. She did not resist, but she kept her eyes on the crowd through the gate.

One of the guards had followed Graves. "But what if they actually attack, sir?" he asked. He looked nervously over his shoulder at the mob, now less than twenty-five yards down the road, and advancing slowly.

Graves looked at him. "Fire warning shots over their head — unless they actually touch the fence."

The guard waited for Graves to go on. When it was evident the SIS man was not going to say anything else, the guard shook his head. "But what if they do storm the gate, sir? What then? Am I supposed to shoot into the crowd?" He looked again at the people. "Hell, there're women back there. Maybe some children too. Am I supposed to shoot at them?"

Graves was an old hand in the service. He was not going to be caught so easily. "Look," he said. "This base has to be defended; you know that."

"Yes, sir," the guard nodded nervously.

"Then defend it. Do whatever you think is necessary."

"Including shooting into the crowd?"

"Whatever you think," Graves said.

"Shit," the guard swore, and he turned away, understanding full well that if he did the wrong thing it would be his ass and no one else's.

Graves got into the jeep and started the engine. He did not switch on the headlights. "Just hold them here for a little while," he shouted to the guards. "I'll be right back."

He turned around and drove quickly up the hill past the administration building to his barracks. He helped Gloria out of the car, and upstairs to his room, where he showed her the shower.

"Get cleaned up. I've got to talk to Mr. Webb. When I get back I'll bring some clothing for you."

She nodded uncertainly.

"Are you hungry?"

She shook her head, and shuddered, as if even the thought of eating something was revolting to her.

"I'll be back in a few minutes. You just hang on here," Graves said. He headed for the door, but Gloria stopped him.

"What about Blake? Are we going into town for him?"

Graves looked at her. But then he nodded. "Sure. Sure," he said. I'll be right back." He turned and went out the door, hurried downstairs, and rushed across to the administration building.

Inside, Bower's office was lit up, but deserted. No one was in the outer offices either.

Back outside, Graves hurried over to the workshops and supply areas where the technicians had been working, trying to rig the antenna and a transmitter so that they could communicate with the outside. There was no one there, either.

Graves hurried out of the main workshop and looked around. There was no one here. No one on the base.

A gunshot came from the area of the main gate, and a huge cry went up. Graves took a few steps that way.

Christ! The townspeople had actually stormed the gate! Graves looked wildly around. It was then that he spotted the large patch of blood in the dirt just at the corner of the workshop.

He went to it, and knelt down. It was blood. He looked up. There was no one around. The attack had come silently while he had been down at the gate. But it had happened so fast it had to mean that they were still here.

Graves raced back across the road to where he had parked the jeep, and pulled his automatic rifle from the back.

Keeping low, and scanning the darkness in all directions, he hurriedly worked his way back to his barracks, and clattered up the stairs to his room, where he barged in.

Gloria Conley, nude, had just stepped out of the bathroom, a towel wrapped around her hair. She looked up, startled.

Graves shut out the lights, plunging the room into darkness except for the bathroom light.

"Shut that out," he snapped. "They're here on the base."

Gloria hurried back into the bathroom and snapped off the light. She came back to where Graves stood by the window looking out across the base. There were several other gunshots from the main gate. Now in the darkness, Graves could make out the muzzle flashes. The sound of the angry crowd, banging and shoving at the fence was clear in the still night air.

It was absolutely dark outside. Graves automatically looked up at the sky. It was overcast; there were no stars whatsoever. Here, at this time of the year, it meant only one thing: Storm. Damn! On top of everything else, they were going to get some weather. Even as he realized it, he heard the ominous rumble of distant thunder.

Gloria shivered. "We've got to get out of here. Now! Blake is in town. We've got to help him."

"The townspeople are here," Graves started, but he stopped short. O'Meara knew what was going on. He'd know how to get out of this situation. If they could get to him, they might have a chance. At least they'd be two men and a woman together.

That was the ticket, he thought. From what he had heard about O'Meara, he was highly thought of. If they pulled this off, it'd be a feather in all their caps. Including his. And this would definitely be his last field assignment. It'd be London with a flat, and the countryside with a lovely old house. He could even get married. Christ! He could almost taste it.

He pushed past Gloria, tore open his closet door, and grabbed a pair of khaki slacks and a short-sleeved shirt, throwing them at her.

"Put these on; we're getting the hell out of here," he shouted.

He rummaged around in the bottom of his closet, coming up with a pair of sandals. He threw them to her. Then he went back to the window, and keeping out of sight looked down across the base.

More thunder sounded, and he could see the flash of lightning. There were more shots from the main gate.

He was less worried about the crowd there, though, than he was about whoever had attacked the base from the cliffs.

It had been silent. Everyone from administration and the supply shacks were gone. He couldn't believe they were dead. But they were simply gone. And there had been no noise. Nothing but the one patch of blood.

Gloria had gotten dressed. She had had to tie his belt around her waist to keep the trousers up. Graves looked at her. She seemed more sexy, more appealing now that she was dressed in his clothing, than she had nude. He couldn't believe it, but he wanted her right then and there.

She stepped back, sensing his mood. A round of gunfire from the direction of the main gate brought him around. And he suddenly felt like a fool. There'd be time later, he told himself. All the time in the world, if they survived.

"Let's get out of here," he said, going to the door.

He threw the door open. A small, compactly built little man, dressed in black pajamas, a long, curved sword in his right hand and a wicked looking dagger in his left, stood there.

Without hesitation, Graves swung his M16 up, thumbed the safety, and before the ninja could bring his sword down, fired off a short burst, catching the man in the thigh, the gut, and across his chest.

The ninja was blown back out into the corridor, bouncing against the far wall. Fearful now, Graves stuck his head out the doorway and glanced both ways up the corridor. There was no one else there. The corridor was quiet.

He looked across at the downed ninja. The man's eyes were open, and there was a determined look on his face.

They were here! They were determined to kill everyone on the base, with the townspeople at the front gate apparently acting as a diversion.

Gloria was right behind him. Together they hurried down the hall, down the stairs, and outside, where they crouched for a moment or two in the shadows of the doorway.

There was a lot of shouting and screaming toward the main gate, but there was no sound elsewhere on the base. Now, knowing why the base was so quiet, it frightened Graves so badly that he was having trouble controlling his muscles. He wanted to run and hide somewhere. He wanted someone to be there for him, to protect him. Of course, none of that was possible, he knew. He was going to have to get the hell away from here, and now. Yet he understood that they were on an island. They could go only so far before all means of escape would be cut off.

Graves stepped out of the shadows and raced across to his jeep. He jumped up behind the wheel and started the engine as Gloria came around and got in on the passenger side.

He handed her the M16. "Do you know how to use one of these?"

Gloria looked at it. Thunder rolled again. She looked up, but then looked back. "I can aim it. I can pull the trigger. What else is there?"

"Nothing," Graves said. He realized that he was beginning to respect her. She had a lot of guts.

He jammed the jeep into gear and took off, wheels spinning, toward the main gate.

"There might be a lot of people still down there," he shouted over at her.

She gripped the automatic rifle a little harder. "If need be, can you shoot?"

"I told you I could," she shouted.

The thunder rolled again, and the first big drops of rain began to fall as the wind began abruptly to gust from the sea.

The shooting had stopped from the area of the main gate, but a huge explosion flashed suddenly in the night sky behind them, a massive fireball rising up into the clouds.

Graves nearly ran the jeep off the road. He pulled up, and swiveled around in the seat to look back. For a second or two, he could not make any sense of it; it was hard to get his bearings in the darkness.

But then he understood what he was seeing. They had gotten the generators and the fuel dump. They had evidently planted charges—or they had simply set fire to everything.

But there'd be no more electricity on this base. Not for a long time to come. Whoever was doing the attacking had made sure of that.

Graves turned back, slammed the jeep into gear again, and they continued toward the gate, going faster and faster, Gloria bringing the M16 up, ready to fire at the first sign of trouble.

At the last moment, Graves flipped on the headlights illuminating the scene of carnage at the gate, which had been shoved in and was laying against the guardhouse, off its hinges.

There were at least a dozen people on the ground. A couple of them were moving around, but most were obviously dead. Among them were the gate guards, their throats slashed.

A couple of bottles and a brick came out of the night at them, but then they were past the wreckage and out on the dirt road without having fired a shot.

Gloria turned in her seat and looked back up at the base. Graves glanced at it in the rearview mirror.

"Is everyone gone now?" she asked.

"I don't know. But I think so," Graves said. Out here, he got a great sense of isolation. He and this woman were utterly alone. And chances were they would not survive.

They had made it to the main highway, and Gloria motioned for Graves to pull up. He did.

"What is it?"

"No one will be in town now," she said. She was looking up the highway in the direction of Taranaga's compound.

"Probably not," Graves said. "There probably won't be anyone left up there, either."

Gloria looked at him. She hopped out of the jeep.

"Hey, wait a second—" Graves shouted. She held him off.

"I'm going back to Taranaga's. I'm taking the

gun. If I can find him, I'll hold him. He might be our ticket out of here. Meanwhile, you can go into town to look for Blake."

Graves looked at her. She was right, of course. The base was under attack. Now was their chance to strike back. But Christ, he didn't want to do this alone.

"Good luck," she said, and before he could say a word she had disappeared into the night, the wind rising stronger, and the rain beginning to fall in earnest.

Fourteen

An explosion sounded from a long way off, between the rumbles of thunder. It was the base. Briggs was certain of it. Taranaga had sent his ninja and his house staff off, and they had attacked the base.

Taranaga laughed. Briggs looked up as the houseboys helped the old Japanese to his feet.

"I am not finished with you, Blake. There will be more," Taranaga said. "Much more. You will beg me to kill you quickly. I promise you that."

The houseboys helped Taranaga totter away, outside of Briggs's limited field of vision where he was tied to the chair.

He heard a door open and close; then there was silence. For several long seconds, Briggs strained to hear if there had been anyone left here with him. If so, he would not have a chance of getting free. As it was, he had nearly loosened the bonds holding his wrists to the point where he could get his hands free.

He groaned. There was no response.

Tensing his muscles, Briggs worked his wrists free and rolled to the right, the chair tipping over with a crash.

But he was alone. Quickly, he undid the ropes that held his waist to the chair, and his legs to the chair legs, and pulled away.

He examined himself. His scrotum was inflamed, and there were blisters on his inner thighs. Every time he moved, the pain shot up into his gut and down to his ankles with excruciating sharpness. But he did not think he would be damaged permanently.

Rolling over, he scrambled to his feet, but he fell down after taking only one step; his legs had simply buckled beneath him, the room spinning.

Christ. He could not go on like this.

He crawled across to one of the sliding doors at the back, listened a moment to make sure no one was on the other side, and slid it open.

It was Taranaga's bedroom, as he had thought it would be. He went inside, sliding the door closed.

A dim light shone from a small stand, and there was incense burning, its odor pleasant, peaceful.

Within a couple of minutes Briggs had found a loincloth, which he tied around his waist. In a drawer of a lacquered chest, he found a stainless-steel dagger. In a larger compartment he found two samurai swords. He grabbed all three weapons and, a little steadier on his feet but still in immense pain, had started for the inner door that led, he suspected, to the corridor that ran the length of this wing, when he spotted his own stiletto on Taranaga's desk.

He grabbed it, but then stopped a moment. This all had been too easy. It was almost as if Taranaga had set this all up. But why? What was the crazy old bastard up to now?

Briggs went to the rear door, where he stopped to listen a moment. There was nothing but the rumble of thunder. Sliding the door open a crack, he looked outside. Taranaga and his housemen had not come back yet.

Turning, he looked toward the inner door. Something was suddenly wrong here. The place was just too quiet. Where the hell had they all gone? Why had they left?

He closed the outer door, and painfully made his way across to the inner door, which he slid open an inch or so.

The corridor was empty, and was deathly still. Only the light from the lightning flashes, coming more and more frequently, provided any illumination.

Briggs took his own stiletto and one of the samurai swords, leaving the other weapons behind, and stepped out into the corridor, hobbling toward the front of the house.

Behind him, screens had been erected to cover the gap caused by the explosion and resultant fire in the armory. But the odor of cordite, and of burned wood and fabric, was very strong. The corridor floor was soaked with water from the fire-fighting efforts.

Halfway to the main section of the sprawling house, Briggs pulled up short, hearing something to his right.

He cocked his head in an effort to hear better, and the sound came again. It was static from a radio. And there was a low murmur of voices.

Gripping his weapons even tighter than before, he shuffled to a rice-paper door and stopped. The sound was coming from inside the room. It was radio static. Someone was talking in Japanese.

Briggs carefully eased the door open a crack and looked inside. Taranaga was there, along with his two houseboys and another man, clad in the black pajamas of the ninja.

They had numbers. But he had surprise.

Briggs slammed open the door and leaped inside; swinging his samurai sword, he decapitated one of the house boys and wounded the ninja slightly on the side.

Taranaga leaped aside, shoved open the door on the opposite side of the room, and slipped outside, while the other houseboy grabbed his sword and brought it around at Briggs, who countered the swing, knocking the blow aside and slicing the man's chest wide open.

The houseboy fell back, but before Briggs could go after Taranaga, the ninja had regained his balance and attacked, nicking Brigg's left arm deeply enough to cause him to drop his samurai sword.

He leaped back as the warrior came in for the kill, bringing his stiletto up in the defensive position. But he was in no condition for the unequal fight. The ninja was in good strength: he was well fed and well rested, and suffered no wounds. Briggs, on the other hand, had lost a lot of blood, two of his ribs were cracked, his upper legs and crotch were painfully burned, and he had not slept or eaten properly in what seemed like weeks.

A second slice, this one on Briggs's knife wrist, made him drop his stiletto. He tried to reach for the blade, but the ninja warrior held him off.

Briggs backed up, and circled to the left, the warrior following him. The man was still wary, even though Briggs was no longer armed. Briggs grinned.

"You can give up now, if you don't want to die," Briggs said.

The warrior hesitated for just a moment, and then had started to leap forward, the samurai sword raised high, as the corridor door slammed all the way open.

Briggs and the Ninja looked as Gloria Conley, dressed in some sort of khaki uniform that was miles too big, stepped around the corner. She carried an M16 automatic rifle, which she brought around to bear on the ninja.

"Hai," she screamed, and fired a long burst that caught the warrior across the chest and face, some of the bullets whistling by Briggs's head, others tearing up the far wall.

The ninja was thrown backward off his feet, blood flying everywhere, through the rice paper and wood-framed wall into a rock garden.

Briggs was rocked back by the intensity of her attack. She dropped the rifle and leaped into the room to him.

"You're alive! You're alive!" she cried, crashing into Briggs.

They went down together in a heap, the pain from his wounds and injuries nearly blowing the top of his skull off, causing him to black out momentarily.

". . . Blake? Mr. Blake. . . ?"

Someone was shouting at him, from a very long ways off. Briggs knew it was important that he should understand, and he forced himself out of the deep, black hole into which he had fallen. He opened his eyes, and looked into Gloria's face, a deeply concerned expression in her eyes.

He reached up and touched her. "It's all right," he mumbled.

"Oh . . . God, what is it?" she said.

"I'm all right," he said.

She pulled him up, and the pain was so intense that a cry escaped his lips. He swooned and fell back, the room spinning nauseatingly.

Gloria was above him again, saying something, and then she was pushing his legs apart. "Oh, God," she cried. But then she seemed to be gone.

For a long time, the pain throbbing throughout his entire body, Briggs was content to lie as he had fallen, without moving a muscle. But then Gloria was back, with a large case that she set down beside him.

"They attacked the base," she said, opening a jar of salve, and pulling out a thick wad of cotton. "Mr. Graves helped me escape. I think we were the only two to get off that base alive."

She touched his inner thigh with the salve, and

for just an instant the pain nearly caused Briggs to black out again, but then, where she had touched, the pain suddenly began to subside.

"This is a local anesthetic cream," she said. "It is very good." She continued daubing the salve on his burns. "What in God's name did he do to you?"

"The base," Briggs said through gritted teeth. "Did they get a message out?"

"I don't think so," Gloria replied, looking up. "Are you going to be all right?"

"I think I'll be able to manage," he said. "Everyone on the base is dead?"

"That's what Mr. Graves told me," she said, finishing with his burns. She wrapped his legs lightly with gauze, and then helped him sit up.

"I'm going to need some clothing," he said.

"I'll get it," Gloria said. She jumped up and disappeared down the corridor.

Briggs wrapped a bandage tightly around his cracked ribs, and by the time Gloria had returned with fresh khakis he was on his feet, checking out the radio gear. Her wild shooting, though, had ruined most of the equipment. A couple of the grounds monitors were still operative, but nothing else seemed to work. There was a strong smell of burned electrical insulation.

Gloria helped him pull on the clothing, including a pair of boots she had found for him.

"There was no one left on the base?"

"I don't know," Gloria said. "Mr. Graves went into town to look for you. We weren't sure where you were."

Briggs scooped up the M16 from where Gloria had dropped it and checked the clip. It was still nearly half-full. Not much, but it was better than nothing.

He stepped to the door through which Taranaga had disappeared in the fight, and looked out into a narrow courtyard. There was a gate on the opposite side.

Briggs stepped into the rain and, careful to present only a narrow target of himself, peered out the gate.

There was nothing but the dark jungle leading up toward the volcano. Briggs stepped through the gate, Gloria behind him.

"He went this way," Briggs said. "Probably is hiding up in the hills somewhere."

"He goes up there all the time," Gloria said.

Briggs turned around. "What?"

"He goes up there every day sometimes. But it's taboo."

"What's up there? Has he got a place. More warriors?"

"I don't think there is anyone up there. I think it has something to do with the war. He was on this island before and during the war, you know. He was a young lieutenant, and he was the island commander."

"Was there fighting here?"

"No, I don't think so. At least he never talked about it."

As much as he wanted to go after Taranaga at this moment, he had to find out about the base. And then about Graves. He could not just leave them.

He turned, and went with Gloria across the courtyard back into the house. After a quick search, he found a flashlight and stuffed it in his pocket.

"Was there anyone around when you came in?" he asked.

"I didn't see anyone until I found you and the others," she said. "I think the compound is deserted. They're all at the base."

"But if they've overrun the base, they'll be coming back here?"

"I think so," Gloria said, fearfully.

"Do you know if there are any weapons here?"

She shook her head.

"Damn," Briggs swore, his mind racing. They didn't have a lot of time left. "How about cars, or jeeps—anything like that?"

She shook her head. "They're all gone, or they're destroyed out front. There was a big accident and a fire."

"I know," Briggs said. "How about gasoline? Where did they get their gasoline?"

"In town at the depot."

"There is no gas here?"

"Yeah, sure. There's an underground tank, out near the gate. Near one of the maintenance sheds."

Briggs suddenly knew what he was going to do. It wouldn't be very pretty, but there was nothing else. "One last question," he said.

Gloria looked into his eyes. She was frightened.

"When they come back . . . when Taranaga's

warriors return, how do they come?"

She shrugged. "Through the main gate. It's the only easy way in or out."

"Come on," he said grimly. "We've got some killing to do."

Briggs hobbled down the corridor, across the mostly ruined main room through which he had driven the truck, and out across the compound, Gloria right behind him.

"What do you mean, killing?" she asked. "What are you talking about?"

"This is an island," Briggs said. "We've got nowhere to go. If Taranaga's people have killed everyone out at the base, they'll be coming after us. They'll never let us go free."

"But . . . we've only got the one gun."

"Right—" Briggs had started to say, when he heard something on the wind and stopped short, cocking his head so that he could hear better.

"What is—?" Gloria started, but Briggs motioned for her to be silent. Then she heard it too. Her eyes went wide and she stepped back, her hand going to her mouth.

"They're coming back already," Briggs said. "We've got to hurry!" He raced the rest of the way across the compound, mindless of his painful injuries, Gloria in a dead run just barely able to keep up with him.

They got to the maintenance shed. The gate, which Briggs had crashed through with the truck earlier in the evening, lay up against another shed across the path.

The gas pump was secured with a heavy padlock. Briggs handed his rifle to Gloria, then pulled out his stiletto and began work on the lock.

They could hear the crowd very plainly now. The wind was coming from that side of the island and their voices carried a long way. Yet Briggs knew they were very close. To be caught here like this now would mean certain death for both him and Gloria. And Taranaga would make sure their deaths would not be clean or pretty.

"Mr. Blake?" Gloria said anxiously.

"Hold it . . ." Briggs said; then he had the last tumbler and the lock snapped open.

He sheathed his stiletto, pulled the lock off, and tossed it aside. He pulled the pump nozzle off its hook, turned the pump on, and extended the hose as far as it would go.

"What are you doing?" Gloria asked urgently.

"Stand back," Briggs said. He squeezed the trigger, the gas spurting out of the nozzle full force and locked the mechanism in place.

Working back and forth, as if he were watering his lawn, Briggs sprayed the entire entryway to the gate with gasoline. Gallon after gallon spurted from the hose, building up in puddles in the hollows, and running off into the jungle and the road from the high spots.

Gloria looked up as the noise of the approaching crowd got louder, then at Briggs and the gasoline, and suddenly she understood.

She stepped back a couple of paces. "Oh . . . my God . . . they'll all be burned alive . . . No!"

Briggs laid the still gushing nozzle in the middle of the driveway and stepped back away from it.

The gasoline smell was very strong now; it pervaded the night air — but most of the odor was blowing back up into the compound, away from the road below.

Briggs took the M16 from Gloria and together they fell farther back, off into the woods toward the southwest fence.

They pulled up short just within the shadows, and Briggs released the safety catch on the M16 after making sure there was a round in the chamber.

"You can't do this," Gloria said.

Briggs turned to her. "It's them or us," he said harshly. "Do you think they gave anyone out at the base a chance?"

"But . . ."

Briggs turned back, brought the rifle up so that it was propped against the bole of a tree, and took aim on the gas pump.

The first of the black-clad ninja warriors, flushed with their easy victory, came through the gate and stopped there, trying to step around the gasoline.

More and more of the ninja and townspeople and Taranaga's staff crowded through the gate. There was a babble of shouts and questions.

Briggs fired a shot that hit the gas pump. Nothing happened.

More and more people were crowding through the gate. A half-dozen of the ninja, realizing what must be happening, raced directly away from the still gushing gasoline.

"No," Gloria screamed. She shoved at Briggs

just as he was squeezing off his second shot. It went wide.

He shoved her aside.

Three of the ninja had reached safety when Briggs took aim a third time; he squeezed off another shot.

For a long, terrible moment Briggs did not think this one had worked either, but then it was as if a lightning bolt had struck the gas pump. There was a very large crash, and a huge tongue of flame leaped from the tank to the nozzle, and then directly into the middle of the crowd.

In the next instant, the entire entryway and road to the compound lit up in a huge fireball, the warm concussion rolling back, knocking the ninja who had escaped off their feet, and flattening some of the trees near where Briggs and Gloria were crouched.

Gloria screamed. Briggs's stomach was churning over and over. He kept telling himself that it had been them now or the killing would've continued. It was not he who had brought this about. It had been Taranaga.

He turned around. Gloria had shrunk back. "My God, you're worse than he is!" she cried.

There were only a few screams from the gate, which quickly died out. Most of the people had mercifully been killed in the initial blast. Briggs did not feel very good about it, no matter what the justification had been.

He looked back. The ninja who had escaped the blasts were recovering from the concussion and falling back from the intense heat. He brought up the M16, took aim, and squeezed off a shot, dropping one of the ninja warriors.

He pulled around to the next one, but the others had scattered, dodging back and forth as they ran, keeping very low.

Briggs squeezed off two more shots, but they went wide.

He turned back to Gloria, but she was gone. He shook his head. It was just as well, he told himself. He had one thing left to do now. He looked up toward the hills and the volcano on the other side of the compound. Taranaga was up there somewhere. Taranaga and the answers to why all of this had happened.

Fifteen

Keeping low and well within the shadows of the jungle at the fringe of the compound, Briggs moved fast, circling behind the house to where he had found the gate leading to the path into the hills. From time to time he stopped and tried to spot the ninja who had survived the fiery blast, but there was nothing to see.

The wind continued to rise, and it rained harder, crashes of thunder closely following the lightning bolts illuminating the entire jungle as the storm intensified.

He hoped that Gloria could keep out of harm's way until he came back for her, and that Graves, with luck, could figure out how the phone system in town worked.

He still wasn't quite sure about the SIS man. All along, this business could have been stopped if he had only gathered the proof he needed to present to

Hope-Turner. Christ, conclusive proof was all around.

Graves, he suspected, was much like Hope-Turner in many ways. Both men were good at their jobs, but both were more interested in advancing their careers; neither of them wanted to step on toes. And stepping on Taranaga's toes, had the man been innocent, could have had worldwide repercussions.

On balance, Briggs found that he really couldn't blame Graves for his overcautiousness. He seemed to have come through all right at the end. Or at least according to Gloria.

Briggs reached the back of the house, locating the gate almost immediately, and across from it the path that led up into the hills, and the volcano beyond.

He looked back toward the house as lightning lit up the night sky, with the heavy crash of the thunder moments later. The storm was still building. Torn between leaving Gloria with the ninja, and settling this entire business once and for all, he hesitated.

Deciding, he turned and headed up the path, keeping low and moving as fast as he dared along an unfamiliar track. From this point on, he was definitely on Taranaga's private domain.

The path climbed abruptly at first, but then leveled out for a quarter mile. Briggs stopped once, thinking he heard something on the wind between thunder. But he wasn't sure at all, and he continued.

It was raining very hard at the upper elevations, and Soshi Taranaga, nearly at a state of collapse, was soaked to the skin, and covered with mud. He worked feverishly, digging up the shallow grave that had first been dug what seemed like yesterday, but in actuality had been back in 1964.

It all came back to this, in the end. Random thoughts crossed his mind, but they were all one thread in common, even though they were, for the most part, different; and that was how quickly more than forty years had passed.

Taranaga hated all things western, but like any good commander he had taken the time to learn about his enemy. Some western philosopher had once remarked that inside every seventy-year-old was the mind of a twenty-five-year-old.

He felt that now as a sense of frustration, that he could not make himself move any faster, any more efficiently. Already, though, he was in a state of near-collapse. He could not go on much longer. And yet he had to finish before his terrible secret was discovered.

He stopped a moment and looked down the hill, but he could see nothing in the dark, blowing rain. The explosion in the compound below could only have meant that somehow the man who identified himself as the Canadian journalist had gotten free, and had caused a considerable amount of damage. Taranaga had instinctively known the man would cause this trouble. He had known it, and yet he had been powerless to stop the outcome!

Turning back to the job at hand, Taranaga looked down into the open grave, which was illuminated momentarily by a bright flash of lightning.

Had he made a mistake after all? he asked himself. Had it all been the result of a foolishly naïve decision back in the thirties, that he had perpetuated by an intransigence that would not allow him to change course? Had he been a stupid young man who had grown into a foolish old man?

He shook his head impatiently: He was tired, he was hungry, he was cold, and he was in pain. Most of all, he was frightened.

There was a lot of water in the grave, but Taranaga pushed himself to complete his task. If this was ever found, not only would his life be over, his entire life's work would become forfeit. All of Japan would be made to suffer by the Americans. The world would not soon forget.

"*Haaiii*," he cried in anguish into the falling rain. What had he done?

The rusting old tin can with a couple of pebbles in it rattled a few yards down the hill from him, and Taranaga's heart nearly stopped.

Someone was coming! Someone was on the path! They were coming here!

He tossed the shovel down, grabbed his loaded M16, and hurried down the hillside to where the tin can was hinged on a stick, a thin black wire leading down the hill to the path.

The wind had not rattled the can. Someone was coming up the hill!

For a moment he thought about heading partway down the path and laying in ambush for the Canadian. But he realized how useless that was. Even if he was successful, there would be others. And more and more. His life was over here.

Taranaga looked back up the hill. His secret would come out. There was no hope for it now. He turned, and in a few steps was back on the path that led the rest of the way up the hill to the cave. But then he stopped.

No matter what happened, if he destroyed the Canadian and if he destroyed . . . what was up in the grave . . . no one would really know what had happened here; what had gone on here since before the war. There'd be a lot of guesses. But no one would know for sure.

He looked again down the hill. That was it, he thought. His world might be ending, but no one on the outside would ever know for sure what had gone on here. He would make sure of that.

The wind blew up from the sea, moaning around the cliffs, bending the palm trees nearly down to the ground. Briggs stopped to catch his breath as a flash of lightning lit up the wild night. The thunder rolled in from the west, and when it died he was sure that he could hear the baying of hunting dogs in the distance. It was a sound he had been hearing for the past ten minutes.

Taranaga had sent his ninja warriors after him, in town and the base, and now that he had come this far they'd never let him go.

He pushed away from the bole of the tree he had been leaning against, and continued up the side of the steep hill that rose away from the cliffs lining the island's edge. The evening was hot, despite the gale-force wind. This was just the beginning, he suspected. Soon the monsoon rains would come, making it impossible for anyone to get on or off the island for the duration.

As he ran and stumbled through the darkness, his sweat mingling with the rain, he kept thinking that all of this—everything that had happened—had been for nothing. All the deaths, all the anguish, all of it had been nothing more than the mechanizations of a crazy old Japanese man who was still living his life forty years back.

That thought kept running through Briggs's mind as the only logical, rational explanation for what had happened . . . for what had been happening here apparently since before the Second World War.

He was stopped again near the crest of one of the foothills when an animal leaped out of the darkness onto his back, knocking him forward on his hands and knees.

It was a huge Doberman, its sharp teeth flashing in the lightning, its muscles straining for the kill. It meant that the other dogs he had been hearing could not be too far back, nor could the ninja be far behind.

The animal was going for Briggs's throat, as it had been trained to do. It was very strong, and very large.

Briggs managed to roll over, grabbing his razor-sharp stiletto from its sheath at the small of his back.

The dog was all over him, biting, clawing, growling, drawing blood from a dozen wounds, its powerful jaws ready to close around Briggs throat, ready to kill.

Briggs brought the stiletto around, barely holding the powerful animal off with one hand, and he slipped the blade between the animal's ribs, puncturing its heart.

The Doberman howled in outraged pain, and leaped aside, Briggs still holding onto his stiletto. The animal screamed, and ran in circles biting at its own side, until it finally flopped down in the mud, hindquarters twitching in death.

Lightning crashed again as Briggs got unsteadily to his feet. The thunder rolled in, and when it finally died he tried to listen for other dogs. But there was nothing.

He found the M16 in the mud, slung it over his shoulder, and continued up the hill, stumbling off the path almost immediately.

Another flash of lightning momentarily lit up the night sky, and Briggs happened to look up. He saw a mound of dirt. A shovel beside it. Someone had been digging.

He walked forward, the sudden darkness blinding, until he slipped and fell over the dirt mound, and down into a long, narrow hole.

He was in a grave! Someone had opened the grave and started to remove the body when the storm had come, stopping the work. It was Taranaga! It had to be.

In the flashes of lightning, Briggs got on his hands and knees, and pushed back away from the skeleton, something catching in the fingers of his left hand . . . a chain of some sort. A piece of jewelry with a locket.

Briggs stared at the mostly disintegrated skeleton for a long time, then held the locket up to catch the light from the lightning strikes, and opened it.

The locket contained a photograph of a man. To the left was an inscription. He pulled out his flashlight and shined it on the tiny locket.

"No!" he cried into the storm. "No!" It was impossible. Christ. It could not be possible after all these years.

He shined the light down on the skeleton in the grave and shook his head. After all of these years the mystery had finally been solved. Or at least a part of it had.

He looked at the locket again, then switched out the penlight. He glanced up toward the top of the volcano. Taranaga was hiding somewhere up there.

He looked again into the grave. All these years. He knew what he was going to do. He'd have to destroy the skeleton. Get rid of the locket. It would open up too many old wounds; it would cause too much grief.

Had this been found on some deserted island somewhere it would be one thing, but here like this, on an island that had been held by the Japanese since before the war . . .

Briggs shuddered. He had a fair idea of what had happened.

Her plane had crashed in the Pacific, just as everyone had theorized. Only it had crashed here, or very near there, when Taranaga had been a young lieutenant . . . commanding the tiny garrison here.

If she had survived the crash, he had kept her captive here. Good Lord, all those years.

The name on the locket would always be indelibly burned into his mind. It was Amelia Earhart, one of the most famous women in the world. She'd ended her days here.

Briggs pocketed the locket and quickly filled in the grave, mindful for the sounds of the dogs and of the ninja still behind him.

When he was finished, he stumbled back up onto the path, and around the bend to where the path came very close to the edge of the cliffs that fell hundreds of feet into the storm-tossed sea.

He threw the shovel over the cliff, and then took the locket out of his pocket, thought about it a moment, and tossed it into the sea as well.

"Do you think history will be better served this way?" Taranaga shouted from behind Briggs.

Briggs turned around. He could just barely see Taranaga's outline in the darkness a little way up the path. A lightning strike came, and Taranaga suddenly was in full view for just a second. He was dressed in his World War II Japanese uniform. He held a rifle with a long bayonet attached.

"Why?" Briggs shouted.

"She was spying," Taranaga screamed. "She came here in her puny little airplane to spy on us."

"No," Briggs shouted over the wind. "She was flying around the world. She crashed."

"She crashed because she did not know enough to stay away from these islands. We shot her down.'

"My God," Briggs said, half under his breath.

"But she wasn't dead," Taranaga screamed. "Oh, no, I found her, and I hid her. Only my adjutant and first sergeant knew. And they died."

"She was alive?"

"Yes; for a long time I kept her here. I fed her. I made sure she got medicine."

"Why? Why did you do something like that, Taranaga? Why, in God's name!"

"Not in God's name; in the name of the empire.

She was going to tell me the truth before I would release her."

Briggs was afraid to ask the last question. "How long, Taranaga?"

"I didn't kill her," Taranaga screamed. "She tried to kill my people who were caring for her. They killed her in self-defense."

"Was it during the war? Perhaps before the war?"

Taranaga laughed insanely. "Which war?" he shouted. "She lived, she lived."

"For how long, you bastard!" Briggs screamed.

"For twenty-seven years I kept her alive! Until 1964! Twenty-seven years!" Taranaga charged.

Briggs swung the M16 around, flipped off the safety, and pulled the trigger. Nothing happened. The gun had jammed. It was wet, and it had been laying in the mud. It would not fire.

It was too late to do anything but side-step Taranaga's blind charge with the bayonet. The old Japanese slid past Briggs, stumbling, and then he was over the edge of the cliff, his arms flailing, his legs pumping the air, and suddenly he was gone, soundlessly plunging down to the rocks and the sea below.

For a long time Briggs remained where he had slumped down in the mud, the rain streaming, the lightning crashing all around him.

He thought he heard the dogs, and then he was certain he heard the sounds of intense gunfire, but the wind was now blowing the sounds away from him, and he could not be certain of what he heard.

It was finally over. Taranaga was dead. The grave

was covered, and the locket was destroyed.

It would be years and years, if ever, before the grave might be discovered. And even then there would not be anything to learn from it. By then, with luck, the bones would be mostly disintegrated.

The secret would be safe here for all time. A new satellite receiving station would be built, and within a year a visitor would never know what had happened here.

Someone crashed through the jungle just off the path. Briggs grabbed for his stiletto and had started to swing around when Steve Graves emerged onto the path, Gloria Conley directly behind him. They both were armed with M16s.

"You're alive!" Graves shouted.

"Oh . . . God," Gloria screamed. She looked wildly around. "What happened? Where is Taranaga? Didn't you find him?"

Briggs looked tiredly at the cliff, and then back. Graves understood.

"I caught up with him here. He had a bayonet. He tried to charge me," Briggs said.

Gloria suddenly understood. "He went over the cliff?"

Briggs nodded, and then he got to his feet.

"Thank God," Gloria said, sagging into Graves's arms.

"What was the shooting?" Briggs asked. "And where'd you get the weapons?"

"After I dropped Gloria off, I went into town. The place was deserted; they were all out at the base. The hotel was burned, and so were most of the buildings downtown, but the telephone exchange and the supply depot were both intact. I found the weapons in the supply shed. A consignment to Taranaga."

"Did you get a message out?"

"Sure," Graves said. "The cut-key had been switched off. I switched it back on, and the operators routed me through Port Moresby, to Darwin and then London on the satellite."

"You called London?" Briggs asked incredulously.

Graves nodded. Gloria looked at him with real respect in her eyes.

"Talked to the O.D., who put me through to Hope-Turner himself. They're sending the Royal Marines out here. Should be along by air as soon as the storm lifts. They've even got a sub on its way in case this weather keeps up."

Briggs sighed deeply.

"What happened here?" Graves asked. "Why was the old madman running up here? Did he have something hidden?"

"No," Briggs said tiredly. "He was just running."

"He came up here all the time," Gloria said.

"To be alone on the mountain top. From here you would be able to see the entire island during the day. This was his domain."

"And that was it?" Graves asked.

Briggs nodded.

"All the death and destruction, all that for nothing?"

"He was the commander of the Japanese installation here during the war. He was still living forty years in the past."

"The crazy bastard," Graves said.

"But it's over now?" Gloria asked. "There'll be no

more killing?"

"Not unless there are more of his ninja running around," Briggs said.

"No," Graves replied grimly. "We started up the hill after you when I got back here. We caught up with them and their dogs a half-mile back."

"Then it's over," Briggs said tiredly. "It's time for me to go back home."

"Canada?" Gloria asked.

Briggs shook his head. "No. A little place outside London called Tunbridge-Wells."

Epilogue

It had been two long, very empty weeks since he had been flown off the island and brought back to London for his debriefing.

Rudyard Howard had come over from the States to get in on the act, and along with Hope-Turner and his hatchet people, they had taken Briggs backward and forward over the entire scenario.

Briggs, Steve Graves, and Gloria Conley, were housed in a compound behind a large estate just outside London. Briggs suspected the place belonged to Hope-Turner, but no one ever really said.

The meals were good, they were allowed out for exercise whenever they wanted, but there were definitely being baby-sat for the duration.

"We just want to get it straight," Hope-Turner had put it at one point. "After all, a lot of our people were murdered on that island. We want to know exactly why."

In the end, though, the hatchet boys, the shrinks who had been brought in as consultants, the archives people, the routine historians — all of them — finally bought the premise that Taranaga was brilliant, though insane. They bought Briggs's premise that the man, as far as his island retreat went, had never gotten out of the forties. It was only happenstance that he was wealthy and could give vent to his insane desire that his island not be built upon.

But then in the end it was over. Howard went back to the States, saying nothing about Briggs remaining behind. Hope-Turner went back to Whitehall to pursue other guys in black hats.

Steve Graves and Gloria went off for a holiday in Paris and Rome — no more palm-lined islands for them — and Sir Roger Hume invited Briggs out to Tunbridge-Wells for, as he put it: "a day, a week, or however long."

Coming up the long drive now to Sir Roger's estate just outside the small town, Briggs's stomach was tied in knots, and his heart was hammering. He was frightened.

Of what, he asked himself? Of rejection — or of acceptance?

Briggs looked out across the pastures for a sign of Sylvia riding one of the horses. But there was no one out there, and they drew up to the house, where the driver left Briggs and his bags.

The house staff came out and took Briggs's things, and Sir Roger greeted him at the door.

"Donald, my boy, welcome back . . . welcome back," the old man said, shaking his hand and clapping him on the back.

"It's good to be back, sir," Briggs said. "Out of the fray, so to speak."

Sir Roger looked at him through shrewd old eyes. "I don't quite know if you're out of the fray yet, though, my boy." He smiled wryly, and shook his head.

"Sir?" Briggs asked, confused.

"She's in the back yard, by the pond," Sir Roger said. "She's been on pins and needles for the past two days, ever since she learned you would be coming out here."

"I . . ."

"Go to her, boy—either that or turn around and run as fast as your legs will carry you. But don't sit on the fence, for goodness sake."

"Yes, sir," Briggs said grinning. He hurried through the house, out the back door, down off the broad porch, and halfway across the yard he pulled up short.

Sylvia Hume, dressed in a lovely summer-print dress, off one shoulder, her lovely legs bare, stood looking pensively into the pond. The sunlight in her hair and on her skin made her glow as if she were an angel.

Sensing someone behind her, Sylvia turned around.

For along time they stood looking at each other, each afraid to move lest they ruin an absolutely perfect moment, each afraid that the other would bolt, each so very much in love with the other.

But then she started, and he leaped forward to meet her halfway, taking her in his arms, swinging her off her feet, holding her so very close.

"Briggs, Briggs," she shouted.

"I love you, Sylvia Hume," he heard himself say.

"Oh, God, you've finally said it!" she screeched. "Briggs, I love you so."

"I'll never leave you again," he was saying.

She smiled, looking deeply into his eyes. "You never really left me from the first moment we met, you know. So I don't suspect you'll be leaving me now, no matter where you're off to."

They kissed then, with all of their might, totally oblivious to anything or anyone around them.

Sir Roger had shamelessly come to the back door. He stood watching them, a tear glinting in his eye as he thought about his long-dead wife. "Grandchildren," she had always said. "With grandchildren you'll never be lonely."

THE BEST IN SUSPENSE FROM ZEBRA

THE DOOMSDAY SPIRAL (1481, $3.50)
by Jon Land
Tracing the deadly twists and turns of a plot born in Auschwitz, Alabaster — master assassin and sometime Mossad agent — races against time and operatives from every major service in order to control and kill a genetic nightmare let loose in America!

THE LUCIFER DIRECTIVE (1353, $3.50)
by Jon Land
From a dramatic attack on Hollywood's Oscar Ceremony to the hijacking of three fighter bombers armed with nuclear weapons, terrorists are out-gunning agents and events are outracing governments. Minutes are ticking away to a searing blaze of earth-shattering destruction!

VORTEX (1469, $3.50)
by Jon Land
The President of the US and the Soviet Premier are both helpless. Nuclear missiles are hurtling their way to a first strike and no one can stop the top-secret fiasco — except three men with old scores to settle. But if one of them dies, all humanity will perish in a vortex of annihilation!

MUNICH 10 (1300, $3.95)
by Lewis Orde
They've killed her lover, and they've kidnapped her son. Now the world-famous actress is swept into a maelstrom of international intrigue and bone-chilling suspense — and the only man who can help her pursue her enemies is a complete stranger ...

DEADFALL (1400, $3.95)
By Lewis Orde and Bill Michaels
The two men Linda cares about most, her father and her lover, entangle her in a plot to hold Manhattan Island hostage for a billion dollars ransom. When the bridges and tunnels to Manhattan are blown, Linda is suddenly a terrorist — except *she's* the one who's terrified!

Available wherever paperbacks are sold, or order direct from the Publisher. Send cover price plus 50¢ per copy for mailing and handling to Zebra Books, Dept. 1593, 475 Park Avenue South, New York, N.Y. 10016. DO NOT SEND CASH.

THE BLACK EAGLES
by John Lansing

#1: HANOI HELLGROUND (1249, $2.95)
They're the best jungle fighters the United States has to offer, and no matter where Charlie is hiding, they'll find him. They're the greatest unsung heroes of the dirtiest, most challenging war of all time. They're THE BLACK EAGLES.

#2: MEKONG MASSACRE (1294, $2.50)
Falconi and his Black Eagle combat team are about to stake a claim on Colonel Nguyen Chi Roi — and give the Commie his due. But American intelligence wants the colonel alive, making this the Black Eagles' toughest assignment ever!

#3: NIGHTMARE IN LAOS (1341, $2.50)
There's a hot rumor that Russians in Laos are secretly building a nuclear reactor. And the American command isn't overreacting when they order it knocked out — quietly — and fast!

#4: PUNGI PATROL (1389, $2.50)
A team of specially trained East German agents — disguised as U.S. soldiers — is slaughtering helpless Vietnamese villagers to discredit America. The Black Eagles, the elite jungle fighters, have been ordered to stop the butchers before our own allies turn against us!

#5: SAIGON SLAUGHTER (1476, $2.50)
Pulled off active operations after having been decimated by the NVA, the Eagles fight their own private war of survival in the streets of Saigon — battling the enemy assassins who've been sent to finish them off!

#6: AK-47 FIREFIGHT (1542, $2.50)
Sent to stop the deadly flow of AK-47s and ammunition down the Ho Chi Minh trail, the Black Eagles find the North Vietnamese convoys so heavily guarded it seems a suicide mission. But the men believe in their leader Falconi, and if he says they can do it, by God they'll do it!

Available wherever paperbacks are sold, or order direct from the Publisher. Send cover price plus 50¢ per copy for mailing and handling to Zebra Books, Dept. 1593, 475 Park Avenue South, New York, N.Y. 10016. DO NOT SEND CASH.

THE SAIGON COMMANDOS SERIES
by Jonathan Cain

#2: CODE ZERO: SHOTS FIRED (1329, $2.50)
When a phantom chopper pounces on Sergeant Mark Stryker and his men of the 716th, bloody havoc follows. And the sight of the carnage nearly breaks Stryker's control. He will make the enemy pay; they will face his SAIGON COMMANDOS!

#3: DINKY-DAU DEATH (1377, $2.50)
When someone puts a price on the head of a First Cavalry captain, Stryker and his men leave the concrete jungle for the real thing to try and stop the assassin. And when the bullets start flying, Stryker will bet his life — on the SAIGON COMMANDOS!

#4: CHERRY-BOY BODY BAG (1407, $2.50)
Blood flows in the streets of Saigon when Sergeant Mark Stryker's MPs become targets for a deadly sniper. Surrounded by rookies, Stryker must somehow stop a Cong sympathizer from blowing up a commercial airliner — without being blown away by the crazed sniper!

#5: BOONIE-RAT BODY BURNING (1441, $2.50)
Someone's torching GIs in a hellhole known as Fire Alley and Sergeant Stryker and his MPs are in on the manhunt. To top it all off, Stryker's got to keep the lid on the hustlers, deserters, and Cong sympathizers who make his beat the toughest in the world!

#6: DI DI MAU OR DIE (1493, $2.50)
The slaughter of a U.S. payroll convoy means it's up to Sergeant Stryker and his men to take on the Vietnamese mercenaries the only way they know how: with no mercy and with M-16s on full automatic!

#7: SAC MAU, VICTOR CHARLIE (1574, $2.50)
Stryker's war cops, ordered to provide security for a movie being shot on location in Saigon, are suddenly out in the open and easy targets. From that moment on it's Lights! Camera! Bloodshed!

Available wherever paperbacks are sold, or order direct from the Publisher. Send cover price plus 50¢ per copy for mailing and handling to Zebra Books, Dept. 1593, 475 Park Avenue South, New York, N.Y. 10016. DO NOT SEND CASH.

THE BEST IN ADVENTURE FROM ZEBRA

WAR DOGS (1474, $3.50)
by Nik-Uhernik
Lt. Justin Ross molded his men into a fearsome fighting unit, but it was their own instincts that kept them out of body bags. Their secret orders would change the destiny of the Vietnam War, and it didn't matter that an entire army stood between them and their objective!

WAR DOGS #2: M-16 JURY (1539, $2.75)
by Nik-Uhernik
The War Dogs, the most cutthroat band of Vietnam warriors ever, face their greatest test yet — from an unlikely source. The traitorous actions of a famous American could lead to the death of thousands of GIs — and the shattering end of the ... WAR DOGS.

GUNSHIPS #1: THE KILLING ZONE (1130, $2.50)
by Jack Hamilton Teed
Colonel John Hardin of the U.S. Special Forces knew too much about the dirty side of the Vietnam War — he had to be silenced. And a hand-picked squad of mongrels and misfits were destined to die with him in the rotting swamps of ... THE KILLING ZONE.

GUNSHIPS #2: FIRE FORCE (1159, $2.50)
by Jack Hamilton Teed
A few G.I.s, driven crazy by the war-torn hell of Vietnam, had banded into brutal killing squads who didn't care whom they shot at. Colonel John Hardin, tapped for the job of wiping out these squads, had to first forge his own command of misfits into a fighting FIRE FORCE!

GUNSHIPS #3: COBRA KILL (1462, $2.50)
by Jack Hamilton Teed
Having taken something from the wreckage of the downed Cobra gunship, the Cong force melted back into the jungle. Colonel John Hardin was going to find out what the Cong had taken — even if it killed him!

Available wherever paperbacks are sold, or order direct from the Publisher. Send cover price plus 50¢ per copy for mailing and handling to Zebra Books, Dept. 1593, 475 Park Avenue South, New York, N.Y. 10016. DO NOT SEND CASH.

McLEANE'S RANGERS
by John Darby

#1: BOUGAINVILLE BREAKOUT (1207, $2.50)
Even the Marines call on McLeane's Rangers, the toughest, meanest, and best fighting unit in the Pacific. Their first adventure pits the Rangers against the entire Japanese garrison in Bougainville. The target—an ammo depot invulnerable to American air attack . . . and the release of a spy.

#2: TARGET RABAUL (1271, $2.50)
Rabaul—it was one of the keys to the control of the Pacific and the Japanese had a lock on it. When nothing else worked, the Allies called on their most formidable weapon—McLeane's Rangers, the fearless jungle fighters who didn't know the meaning of the word quit!

#3: HELL ON HILL 457 (1343, $2.50)
McLeane and his men make a daring parachute drop in the middle of a heavily fortified Jap position. And the Japs are dug in so deep in a mountain pass fortress that McLeane may have to blow the entire pass to rubble—and his men in the bargain!

#4: SAIPAN SLAUGHTER (1510, $2.50)
Only McLeane's elite commando team had the skill—and the nerve—to go in before the invasion of Saipan and take on that key Jap stronghold. But the Japs have set a trap—which will test the jungle fighters' will to live!

Available wherever paperbacks are sold, or order direct from the Publisher. Send cover price plus 50¢ per copy for mailing and handling to Zebra Books, Dept. 1593, 475 Park Avenue South, New York, N.Y. 10016. DO NOT SEND CASH.